Zodiac Girls

Discount Diva

Cathy Hopkins

KINGFISHER

Chapter One

The Crazy Maisies

I wish, I wish, I wish I could go, I thought when our form teacher Miss Creighton first made the announcement.

"…I will be taking names from all you Year Eight girls in the next week," she continued. "All those who want to go must register before the end of May which only gives you two weeks."

A school trip to Venice. Four days in sunny Italy. I wanted to go more than anything, ever, since the beginning of eternity and even before that.

"You going to put your name down, Tori?" asked Georgie when the bell went and we headed out of the classroom for the lunch break.

I shrugged my shoulder as if I didn't really care. "Maybe," I said.

"I definitely am," said Megan catching us up and linking arms. "Mum said I could go on the next school trip wherever it was."

"Me too," said Hannah linking arms with Megan.

"Me too," said Georgie. "Which means you *have* to

5

come, Tori. It wouldn't be the same without you. The Crazy Maisies hit Europe."

Me, Hannah, Megan and Georgie. We called ourselves the Crazy Maisies. My mum used to call me that when I was little and acting daft. Me and my mates act daft a lot hence the name.

"Venice isn't *that* great," I said. "Too many tourists. Florence is much more interesting." Hah. Like I'd been to either of them. Not. But I had heard my well travelled Aunt Phoebe saying that Venice was so full of tourists these days that you could hardly move.

"You *have* to come," said Hannah. "And so what if there are loads of tourists? We'll be four of them!"

"Yeah," said Georgie. "Italy here we come."

I felt a sinking feeling in my stomach. I was so going to miss out but I could never tell them the real reason why I couldn't go.

"Si signora, pasta, cappuccino, tiramisu," I said, trying to remember all the Italianish words I had ever heard and to distract them from trying to persuade me to go. I'd have to think up some excuse that they'd all buy later.

"Linguine, Botticelli, spaghetti…" Megan joined in.

"Da Vinci, Madonna, pizzeria, Roma," said Hannah.

Then they started singing a song that we'd done in music class last term. We'd had a supply teacher who had us singing songs from around the globe. "Trying to broaden your horizons," he said as he taught us folk songs from Italy to Idaho. By the end of term however, I think he was glad to broaden his horizons and move onto another school where the pupils weren't tone deaf.

"When the moon hits your eye like a great pizza pie, it's *amore...*" my mates chorused off-key and in terrible Italian accents.

A few girls from Year Nine sloped past and looked at us as if we were bonkers. I play acted that I wasn't with them but Georgie dragged me back and Hannah and Megan got down on their knees, put their hands on their hearts and continued hollering away at the tops of their voices.

Mad. They all are. And they'll have a great time in Venice that's for sure. Another thing that was for sure was that no way would I be going with them. Not a hope in hell.

In the break, we went out into the playground, found a bench on the sunny side and did each other's hair. When we first met, only Georgie, out of the four of us, had long hair. After a short time hanging out together, we all decided to grow it to the same length so that we could play hairdressers and long hair is best for experimenting with. Georgie and Meg are blonde although Megan's hair is thicker and golden blonde whereas Georgie's is fine white blonde. Hannah and I have standard brown hair although Hannah has had chestnut highlights put in her's lately. It looks totally cool. I'd love to have highlights but that's another thing to add to the "not going to happen unless Mum wins the lottery" list.

I think Georgie's the prettiest of the four of us although Megan and Hannah are good-looking in their own ways too. Hannah could pass for being Spanish. She has olive skin and amazing dark brown eyes which look enormous when she puts make-up on and Megan has a sweet face, cornflower-blue eyes and a tiny nose like a doll. Out of all of us, boys mostly pay attention to Georgie and me though. Hannah and Megan say it's because I am pretty too but sometimes I wonder if the main reason that boys talk to me is to get in with Georgie.

I'm not huge on confidence in that department. Some days I can look okay, I know I can, but I could look heaps better if I got my hair done properly and bought some fab new clothes and make-up, but I doubt if that's going to happen any time soon. Reason being, my family are broke and a half, so it's hard trying to keep up on the appearance front. Most of my clothes come from second hand shops but I worry that my mates will find out. At school, girls who don't wear the latest designer gear get called Nickynonames because their clothes don't have recognizable labels. Megan, Georgie and Hannah have no idea that I'm Queen Nickynonames.

"I think we should go for a really sophisticated look when we're in Venice," said Megan as she pulled back Georgie's hair and began to braid it.

"No. I think we should wear it loose," said Hannah.

"Yeah," said Georgie. "Loose and romantic looking. There might be some cute Italian boys to flirt with."

Oh no! Boys! Italian boys. I hadn't thought of that. What if one of my mates got a boyfriend and I wasn't there to share it all with them? What if all *three* of them got boyfriends and had their first kiss? It might happen. I've heard that Italy is a really romantic place. Romeo and Juliet happened over there and they were *way* loved up. I've also heard that Italian boys are very hot-blooded. (I'm not totally sure what that means and whether they really do have hotter blood than us on account of living in a hot climate. Whatever.) Apparently they are more forward than English boys who mostly seem more interested in computers than they do in girls. Anyway, I would be left so far behind in the game of lurve. I'd be like Cinderella left at home while everyone else went to the ball. Erk! That would be freaking *tragic*. The Crazy Maisies do everything new together, that way we can talk about it all and see how we all feel.

"Ow," said Hannah with a wince as I brushed her hair up into a ponytail. "You're hurting."

"Sorry," I said, and made myself brush more gently. I didn't mean to take my frustration out on her but all the talk for the next few weeks would be about the trip. And then they'd go and I'd be on my own. And then they'd come back and all the talk would about the trip again. And I'd have nothing to say because I wouldn't have been there. I'd be left out. It would be awful.

Luckily, Megan changed the subject and began making plans for the weekend. A new comedy movie was on at the local complex. Of course everyone was up for seeing it.

"Brill!" said Georgie. "And we could go for snacks afterwards?"

Megan and Hannah nodded enthusiastically. "Loads of those Mexican spicy cheesy tacos thingees. I luuuurve them."

"Ice cream for me," said Georgie. "Pistachio with… strawberry."

"Pecan fudge is my fave," I joined in.

"We'll have to do the early show, about six o'clock or Mum won't be able to pick me up," said Hannah.

I did a quick calculation as they were discussing how they were going to get there and back and what they were going to eat. I'd need money for the movie. Bus fare. Snack. Coke. Nope. No way I could do it on my pocket money. I get about a quarter of what my mates get and some weeks when things are really tight, Mum can't give us anything at all – us being me, my elder sister Andrea and two brothers William and Daniel. I took a deep breath and got ready to apply my usual philosophy: when the going gets tough, the tough bluff it.

"I can't make it tonight. Mum got me and Dan and Will tickets for the Cyber Queens gig."

"The Cyber Queens? Wow! You *lucky* thing!" said Georgie.

"You've kept quiet about that this week," said Megan. "Those tickets are like the hottest in town."

Hannah playfully punched my arm. "Yeah. Why didn't you tell us?"

"Mum only told us last night. It was a surprise for when we got home."

"A surprise? That's *so* mint," said Georgie. "She's so cool your mum. I wish my mum did stuff like that. I bet my mum hasn't even *heard* of the Cyber Queens. Can she get the rest of us tickets?"

"Don't think so," I replied. "I think she got the last ones."

"Take your digicamera," said Hannah, "take lots of pics to show us."

"Sure," I said.

I felt guilty when the bell went for afternoon lessons. Not only did I not have tickets for the Cyber Queens but I don't have a digicamera either even though I'd told everyone that my gran had got me one as an early birthday pressie. I lied. I don't really like doing it but sometimes it's necessary. I have to make things up so that they don't think that I'm a total loser. My mates all have rich parents who buy them the latest gear: iPods, mobile phones with cameras, computer games, designer gear. They've all got their own telly *and* their own computer in their bedrooms. I don't have my own bedroom. Not even my own bed. Not really. I have to share a room and a bunk bed with my sister, Andrea. Sometimes I sleep on the downstairs sofa just to get a bit of space although even then I have to share it – with our cats, Marmite and Meatloaf (My brother Will named them. Marmite's black and Meatloaf is a dark tabby.)

Anyway, my mates would surely dump me if they knew the truth about my situation and how poor we really are compared to them. When we first all started hanging out together as a group at the beginning of this year, to put them off coming round, I told them that our house was being decorated from top to bottom, kitchen, bathroom, the lot. I keep telling the girls that we're having "nightmares" with the builders who keep letting us down. It's an expression I've heard their parents use a million times.

So far, they haven't been round a lot but when they have, my excuses have worked because the fact is, our house does look like it's in the middle of being decorated. The walls are patchy with daubs of paint here and there where we decided to try out some paint samples but there wasn't enough dosh to buy the paint. There are no carpets on the stairs. The carpets that are down on the floor are worn. There are floorboards up here and there. The whole place looks like it needs ripping out and redoing from top to toe so my story has never met with any questions.

Sometimes I think that Georgie may have twigged but she's never come out and said anything, not yet anyway. It can be stressful on the rare occasions when the girls do come over as I'm afraid that Andrea, Will or Dan might blow my cover. Instead, I try and make sure that we hang out at Megan, Hannah or Georgie's house. I tell them that the floor's up again or the scaffolding is a bit dodgy or the water's off or something. They're so sympathetic that I feel rotten, especially as Georgie seems to like coming to our house and she always brings something with her like some fab shortbread or expensive choccie biscuits or elderflower juice (my fave).

All my mates are kind. They invite me to sleep over

at their houses when I lay the builder nightmare scenario on really thick – like last week I said that a plumber had caused a burst pipe and there was water everywhere. I like going to Georgie's place the best. It's awesome. They have five bedrooms at her house for just her and her mum. *Five*. And seeing as Georgie is an only child, that means they have three spare. *Three*. I wish I could go and live with her sometimes although I know deep down that I'd miss my family and especially the cats. Her house is like a palace compared to where I live, I feel like a princess when I'm there and her parents never interfere with her life. Not like my home. No privacy there. Not even in the bathroom as there is always someone knocking on the door telling whoever is in there to hurry up.

Some days, like today, being poor sucked. It is Friday. The twelfth of May. The whole world would be out enjoying the early summer sun this evening. Certainly half of our school would be. All down the local cinema complex to watch a movie and hang out. Some of the older girls from our school would also be there, showing off fab new outfits they've just got. There would probably even be some boys there from Marborough High down the road. And I'd have to miss out on the whole outing because I haven't got enough money to go.

As we got up to go back into school, there was a

sudden blast of wind blowing up dust and debris from the playground.

"Woah," said Georgie as her skirt billowed up. "Where's that come from?"

"Dunno," said Meg, "but let's run."

In an instant, more papers and toffee wrappers began to blow in a mini tornado around the playground as pupils headed back inside. A piece of paper flew towards me and stuck to my hand. I flicked it off but it fluttered back again and we all laughed because after I brushed it off for the second time, it seemed to follow me as we headed for the door back into the classrooms. It was dancing along behind me and just before I reached the door, it blew right up until it covered my face so that I couldn't see.

"Bleurgh," I blustered as I pulled it away from my eyes.

"Maybe it's meant for you," said Megan taking the paper away from me. "Let's see what it is."

"Yeah right," I said. "Maybe it's a message from a fairy." I was teasing her because last year, she was into fairies and angels and her bedroom was covered with posters of them.

"What does it say?" asked Hannah.

Megan scanned the paper. "Dear Tori, you are to go to the bluebell dell at midnight on Friday night…"

I punched her arm playfully. I knew she was

making that up. "What does it really say?"

"It looks like some sort of promotion type thing," she replied. "Er… advertising local businesses kind of thing. A beauty salon in Osbury. A café/deli. An astrology site. Stuff like that."

"I'll chuck it," I said and took it to put in the outside litter bin in the corner of the playground. As I threw it away, there was a flash of lightning then a rumble of thunder in the distance. I glanced up. The sky had darkened, threatening sudden rain so I raced back to join the others at the door.

"The fairies are angry that you threw away their business promotion," joked Georgie.

"Yeah right. Fairies and elves are alive and well and have taken over Osbury," I laughed back.

Seconds later, the skies opened and rain pelted down so we darted inside as quick as we could.

"Phew," I said as we raced along the corridors. "Just made it."

As we settled into class, our teacher Miss Wilkins was busy closing the windows that had been open earlier in the morning. The rain continued pouring down and the wind was still whipping up debris outside. As she reached the last window at the back of the class near my desk, a piece of paper blew in the window. It sailed right across the classroom and landed plonk in front of me.

Meg, Hannah and Georgie turned to look. I glanced down. It was the same piece of paper that had been following me in the playground! Beauty salon, deli, astrology website…

Maybe Megan was right and there were fairies and guardian angels out there. Maybe this was a message from one of them in code or something. *Yeah. And I'm the richest girl in the world*, I thought. However, the paper arriving in front of me did make me wonder. I didn't believe in fairyland like Meg but I *did* believe that some things are meant to be. Like fate. Or destiny. And *this* was a coincidence. I couldn't deny that. Maybe it *was* meant for me. I was about to put the paper in my rucksack to look at more carefully later when Miss Wilkins closed the last window and turned back to the class. As she did, she saw the paper that had landed on my desk.

"That rubbish is blowing everywhere!" she said as she picked it up, ripped it into tiny pieces and took it to the front where she put it into the bin. "Such a nuisance."

Oh no, I thought as I watched her do it. *There goes the message about my destiny, straight into the bin!*

Chapter Two

Movie night

"I'm sitting there. I got the DVDs," said Will as he shoved Dan off the most comfortable chair in our living room. It's red and velvety with thick plush cushions. Okay, it's a bit worn on the arms and some stuffing's coming out of it round the back but you can sink right into it like it's made of marshmallow. Will found it on a skip last summer and dragged it back here with the help of a few of his mates.

"No. *I'm* sitting there," Dan insisted. " It's *my* turn. You sat there last night."

After a bit more shoving and pushing, they ended up wrestling on the floor and pulling each other's hair.

"Welcome to my world," I said to no-one in particular. I stepped over them with the pan of popcorn I'd just made and went and sat on the chair in question. "Movie time," I said as I turned on the telly.

They both sat up and stared at me in amazement

when they saw that I was sitting in the prize chair. For a moment, we all looked at each other then burst out laughing. We did look daft. I was dressed in black with a tall hat in a Wicked Witch outfit and Dan and Will were dressed as devils complete with horns and vampire teeth. Dressing up appropriately to watch a movie on a Friday night has been a tradition in our house since we were small. Mum started it and it makes it more fun. We have a huge trunk of assorted costumes that Mum has either made or that have been collected from various jumble sales over the years. Witches, wizards, clowns, gorillas, giant vegetables, you name it and it's probably in the trunk. Aunt Phoebe and Uncle Kev, Aunt Pat and Uncle Ernie have all contributed to the trunk and bring stuff back from holidays abroad. They also like to get in costume if they come over to watch a DVD at our house.

Dan was about to make a dive at me but I grinned at him and held up my magic wand. "Talk to the wand because the face ain't listening."

"But it's *my* turn," he said again.

I almost gave in because he looked put out. But I didn't.

"Life is tough oh small and puny one," I said. (Dan hates being called that as he is quite small for his age.) "I will tell Mum that you bunked off sports practice last Saturday if you don't let me sit here. Now sit on the sofa, shut up and let's watch the DVD."

"You wouldn't."

"Try me."

"It's my chair. I brought it back here so I should be the one to sit in it *all* the time," said Will who looked as if he was about to wrestle me too. I pulled out my blackmail card on him.

"Oh really? Well if you don't let me sit here, I will tell my mate Georgia that you fancy her." (What Will doesn't know is that I have a sneaking suspicion that Georgie fancies him back. I shall save that bit of information for another night when it might come in handy.) Will is a looker. Loads of girls at our school fancy him. He's got typical boy band looks. A handsome face with even features and a slim bod. And no spots (big plus). Even though he's my brother, I can see that he's fanciable. Dan's cute too with a wide mouth and the green eyes that we have all inherited from our mum. Dan'll be a babe magnet when he's older. At the mo though, he's not remotely interested in girls. He thinks they're for pushing, teasing or hair pulling and he hates snog scenes in movies. He says that watching people suck face makes him want to throw up.

Dan shrugged then got up to slump on the sofa and a moment later, Will joined him along with Meatloaf and Marmite who took their places on the boys' knees. The cats like a good movie too.

"Correct response," I said with a big smile. Will stuck his tongue out at me. I love my brothers really and their fighting is rarely serious. Just boys being stupid boys.

I used to wonder how Dad would have dealt with their endless scraps and messing about but I hardly think about him any more. It's a waste of time. He clearly isn't coming back any time soon. He left when I was ten. Went back to Australia leaving Mum with the four of us. She sat us all down after he'd gone and said that it had been on the cards for years (like we didn't already know). No-one was to blame and that they should never have got married in the first place as they were such different types of people (ditto, we could hear their endless rows through the ceiling. They could never agree on anything). I could accept that they were incompatible. I've watched the soaps on telly. I know what goes down but personally I don't see why he had to go quite so far away especially when he had the four of us. If he ever sat an Abandon Your Kids exam, he'd get an A star. Okay, so he didn't get on with Mum but what about Andrea, Dan, Will and I? We got on. Yeah, sometimes he was moody and unpredictable and I didn't like that and I *hated* it when he and Mum argued but he was my dad and you only get one of them. I missed him and when he first went, it hit me hard. I felt like a major reject. Like if my own *dad* didn't want me, then no-one else would.

I don't let myself think about stuff like that any more now though. It hurts too much. I put it in a box in my head and locked it. Mum has been great. She tries really hard but for all her positive attitude, she hasn't found it easy as a single mother. Not enough money. Her sisters Phoebe and Pat and their husbandos have been fab and are in and out most days to lend a hand where they can. I love them a lot and know that they love me too. They don't have kids of their own and have sort of adopted us. When they're around, I don't have that reject feeling. They make me feel like I matter. Dad sends a bit of dosh every now and then but not often because, from his letters, it doesn't sound like he has a job yet. That was one of the major sources of the arguments. Mum worked day and night. Dad talked about it but always seemed to have an excuse as to why it wasn't happening.

"Pass me the DVD remote," I said as I spied it on the table.

"You get it," said Dan. "I'm not your slave."

"Yes, you are," I said.

"Oh for heaven's sake," said Will. He snatched up the remote and passed it to me. "I'll get it. Here. Sometimes you're so lazy, Tori."

"So?" I said and kicked off my shoes. "Lazy is good. Now let the entertainment begin." With a flourish of the remote control, I switched on the DVD. We had popcorn and movies. Aunt Phoebe and Uncle Kev would pop by later with pizzas. It was going to be a fun evening despite my earlier disappointment at not being able to go out with my friends.

On the way home from school, I had decided to make the most of the evening and not to sulk about not being able to go out. I'm not a miserable person usually. Just frustrated sometimes. But no point in dwelling on what can't be changed, I reckoned. Andrea was out at her *book* club sleepover, yes, book club sleepover. She is seventeen years old. It is Friday night and she would rather sit around discussing books at a sleepover than try out new make-up or gossip or talk about boys or watch a good movie. That is how sad my sister is. Sometimes I think she isn't actually one of our family. She doesn't look like the rest of us. She has pale skin and blonde wispy hair and blue eyes. The rest of us are dark with green eyes. So anyway, it was just me and the boys. And the cats (who are also dark with green eyes).

The DVDs that Will had borrowed were horror movies (hence our horror costumes) and as the evening went on we had a good laugh seeing who got spooked the most. It was Dan as usual. He's such a sissy since some old geezer at the local train station told him about Irish banshee ghosts who appear outside people's windows just before they die and wail, "the day is for the living and the night is for the dead."

When he went in to make us some hot chocolate (he *is* our slave as he is the youngest at eleven), Will and I sneaked outside and began wailing outside the kitchen window. It was hysterical. Dan went white and almost dropped the mug he had in his hand. Then Will blew it by laughing and Dan looked out the window and saw us doing our cross-eyed zombie walk around the clothes dryer out there. He wasn't amused.

Personally I don't think there's any such thing as ghosts, banshees or zombies but Dan does and he was really mad at us. He doesn't mind dressing up as a vampire but doesn't like to think there might be a real one behind the privet in our backyard. He stormed upstairs and wouldn't come out of his room. We had to beg him in the end. We had to get down on our knees in the corridor outside the room he shares with Will and plead. He can be stubborn and moody sometimes can Dan. Especially if he thinks people are making fun of him. Aunt Phoebe and Uncle Kev arrived with food supplies soon after and that brought him down. He couldn't resist the allure of a Neptuna four cheeses. And he couldn't help but smile when he saw what idiots they looked in their evil goblin masks.

Mum got home at half past eleven just after Aunt Phoebe and Uncle Kev had left.

"What are you still doing up?" she asked when she saw us all sitting round watching telly. "It's way past your bedtime."

"Oh come on, Mum, it's Friday night. No school tomorrow," said Will.

"And I was waiting up for you," I said and got up from the sofa and gave her a hug. "Let me go and make you a tuna toastie and hot chocolate."

"And me one," said Dan.

"And me," called Will.

"Make your own," I called back as I went into the kitchen and got out mugs for all of us. "And anyway, you've just stuffed your faces with pizza."

I like to make a fuss of Mum when she gets home. She works so hard and she looked tired tonight. She often has lately but then who wouldn't if they had to do three jobs? She has no time to look after her appearance any more and always just shoves her hair back in a band and wears old fleeces and trackie bottoms. I remember years ago when her hair looked well cut and glossy and her clothes were pretty and she wore a bit of jewellery. That was when she only had one job and that was part-time at the library. Now all she does is work. During the daytime on Monday to Friday, she works as a receptionist at the local vet.

Most evenings, she does cleaning jobs for an agency who send her to places like the stadium – which is where she's been tonight. If there's been a big match on, she doesn't get home until one. Tonight though it was the Cyber Queens concert and she will have brought me back tickets as she knows I like to collect rock concert tickets in my scrap book with the green and gold Chinese cover. It wasn't totally a lie that I told Georgie about having tickets. Just that I didn't get them until the show was *over*.

Mum's third job is making cakes for special occasions. She's totally brill at it. She can make whatever anyone wants – like if someone works with computers say, she can make their cake look like a PC. Or if someone is a photographer, she can make the cake look like a camera. She's done Superman cakes for little boys, pink heart cakes for Valentine's Day, cakes like tennis rackets for tennis fans – whatever anyone wants. Sadly she doesn't get much time for this job as the cleaning agency keeps calling.

"So how's your day been?" asked Mum as she picked up the post from the hall table and followed me into the kitchen.

"Okay," I said. I didn't tell her about having to miss out on the Crazy Maisies' movie outing. I didn't want her feeling bad about stuff like that on top of everything else. For a few moments while I made her toastie, I thought about asking if there was the slightest chance that I might be able to go on the school trip if I didn't have any pocket money for the next fifteen years. The look on her face as she opened one of the letters stopped me.

"What is it?" I asked.

She took a deep breath. "Oh, nothing interesting. Another bill."

"Can you pay it?"

She nodded. "Just about. Don't you worry, Tori. We'll get by. We'll survive. We always do."

I couldn't help but sigh as I continued making her supper. Get by. I wished we didn't just have to get by. I wished we didn't just have enough to survive. I wished our family could thrive. I wished Mum could have nice clothes again and not have to work so hard. And music-mad Will could get an iPod and Dan, the bike he's wanted for ages. And I wish I could have things like Megan and Georgie and Hannah. I wanted to go out with them like normal girls my age. *Actually no*, I suddenly thought. *I don't want to be normal. I wanted to be super stonking stupidly rich. I'd even buy Marmalade and Marmite new collars. With diamonds on!*

"What's the big sigh about?" asked Mum who as usual didn't miss a thing. "Everything okay with the Crazy Maisies?"

"Yeah. Fine," I said as I busied myself getting out a

tray. I put all thoughts about Italy out of my mind and arranged the things on the tray so that they looked nice. I've learnt to do this from Mum. She does her best to make the most ordinary things special even if it's only by putting a nice napkin or fresh flower on the dining table.

"By the way," she said with a grin as I put the tray with its folded Christmas paper napkin (it was all I could find) in front of her. "I have something you might just be interested in."

She rummaged about in her bag and produced an envelope and held it out to me. "Here. Tomorrow night at the Bridgewater Hotel out near Osbury, they're hosting a charity event. I have some tickets if you want to go."

I tried to look enthusiastic but a charity event? Big deal. Not.

Mum laughed when she saw my face. "Not just any charity event," she said. "It's a charity ball. Chance to glam up and I know how much you like to do that. All the stars are going to be there. Have a look at the guest list."

I took the piece of paper from her and glanced down. Omigod! Topping the bill were the Dust Babies. Only my favourite band in the Universe. And omigod, omi*god* Alicia Bartley from my favourite soap. And... it can't be... Ewan Gregory from T4. He's sooooo gorgeous. My fantasy boy.

The list went on.

"This is like... *mega*," I finally managed to stutter. "And you're saying that I can go?"

Mum grinned and nodded. "Mrs Jackson, the lady who's organizing it, she's ever so nice, remember her? I did her a swimming pool cake last year for her birthday. She asked me to do some of my special cakes for part of the auction and help her out a bit. She asked if I'd like a couple of free tickets for anyone."

"But Mum this is awesome..." I said as I took in the rest of the names on the A star list.

"I know love," she said. "Charity is big business these days. They all try to attract the big names. And it looks like it will be fun."

"I'll say."

"So you want to go?"

"Er... obvi.'"

Mum smiled happily. "Good. It's about time you had something special to look forward to, Tori."

This is so mint, I thought. *Okay, so Cinderella doesn't get to go to Italy. Or the movies. But she gets to go to the ball. The hottest charity ball in history.* I couldn't wait to tell Hannah, Meg and Georgie.

Chapter Three

Osbury

"Mum will be mad at you if she knows you've been snooping in there," said Will appearing behind me as I was going through Mum's wardrobe on Saturday morning when I thought everyone was out.

I'd had every stitch of clothing that I owned out on the floor in my and Andrea's bedroom. And every stitch that Andrea owned as well as she was out at her chess club. (She really is Queen of Dorksville. Interests: chess, books, science and history. Bleurgh.) After I had exhausted our stuff, I went into look at Mum's.

"But she isn't going to find out, is she?" I said and attempted to grab Will's wrist and give him a Chinese burn. He was too quick for me and jabbed me in the stomach causing me to curl over in pain. Oh the joy of having brothers. I had hoped that he might have grown out of the wanting to torture his little sister phase now that he'd turned fifteen but apparently not.

"What will you give me not to tell her?" asked Will.

"A black eye," I said. "Now go away and leave me alone. I have important business to conduct."

"Like what?"

"Like finding what I am going to wear for this big do tonight. It's hopeless, Will. I may even have to give the ticket to someone else."

"Why? I thought you were over the moon about going – chance to show off and all that."

"I was but oh… you won't understand. You're a boy."

Will surveyed the pile of clothes I'd put on the bed. "I do understand actually. I'm not as stupid as you think. You don't know what to wear and you want to look cool."

Hmm. Maybe he wasn't as stupid as I thought.

"Yeah… well… exactly. It's, like, really important. There will be some awesome people there and you can bet anything they'll be wearing all the latest designer stuff not hand-me-downs that don't fit properly. I've got nothing. I'm such a Nickynonames…"

"Nickynonames?" asked Will.

"Someone who only has uncool clothes, you know, clothes that haven't got a good label, designer gear."

"Oh that. So what? I'd have thought it's whether something looks good or not that counts, not if it's got some posh label on it. You must have something?"

"Not that's posh. Only that silver top that Mum got

me last year from Oxfam but it went all shiny and stretchy in the wash. Oh why can't I have a sister who has style? A sister who has a wardrobe full of fab clothes that I can borrow? She has as much dress sense as a dead dog. I on the other hand have fabulous taste."

"Fabulous doesn't always mean expensive," said Will.

"What do you know?"

"I've got eyes haven't I?" asked Will as he made himself comfortable on Mum's bed. "And I've seen some girls look hot because of the way they wear what they've got on. Not because it cost a fortune. Anyway, why can't you borrow something from one of your rich mates? Georgie looks loaded. I bet she's got piles of clobber. Ask her."

"Once again you poor, challenged-in-the-brain-department person, you don't understand."

"Yes I do. You don't want her to know that we're poor. Don't think I don't know that you're ashamed of who we are and where we live and…"

I felt shocked that he'd think that because not in a million squillion years would I be ashamed of him. "I am not! Shows what you know. Anyway, Mum had two tickets and Andrea wasn't interested in going so she said that I could ask a friend. So I asked Georgie. So there. That's why I don't want to borrow anything from her because she will be wearing her nicest outfit herself."

"Bet she's got loads of other things. And you *are* ashamed of us. I've seen you when you're here with your mates. You can't get them out of the house fast enough."

"I'm *not* ashamed of you, Will. Honest. Not of who you are, just of where we live. I mean look at it…" I said as I indicated the old-fashioned beige wall paper on the wall. "I mean if you saw Georgie's house you'd understand."

Will shrugged. "I have mates who live in posh houses. So what? That's not why I hang out with them. Or them with me."

"Yeah but you're a boy. What do boys care about nice things? All you care about it footie and computer games. For me how things look matters. I thank God for school uniform, I really do. At least we all have to wear the same thing there apart from our trainers."

Will looked at me sulkily. "I don't think you should care about stuff like that. What does it matter?"

"It matters a great deal il stupido, now clear off and leave me alone."

"Hey," said Will as he got off Mum's bed. "If it's a charity ball, why don't you go to a charity shop? You might find something. You never know."

With that he trudged off to his room and after I'd

exhausted Mum's wardrobe, I began to think that his idea wasn't half bad. Sometimes people gave away really nice stuff to charity shops. I wouldn't go to our local shop though. They wouldn't have anything decent. I knew what was in there as all our family were regulars. Mum gets most of our clothes in there, she jokes that she and I are discount divas. Andrea gets books, Will gets DVDs, Dan gets great games and I get some good CDs. But clothes fit for a ball? No chance. The stuff in our local shop was the sort that even the jumble sales didn't want. But there were other charity shops in other areas. Areas where rich people lived. Suddenly I remembered the leaflet that had blown towards me on Friday. For shops in Osbury. It was the village nearest our school. A few new shops had opened there lately and I was sure that one of them was a charity shop.

After leaving a note for Mum, I legged it as fast as I could to the bus stop and took the bus into Osbury. It was the most upmarket village in our area. If there were going to be designer giveaways anywhere then that would be the place.

Half an hour later, I got off the bus and scanned the row of shops opposite the bus stop. *Result!* I thought, *there's the charity shop*.

I was about to make my way over the road when

someone tapped me on the shoulder. I turned to find the most stunning-looking woman I had ever seen. She didn't look like a local, in fact she looked like a celebrity and in her early twenties although I was never very good at judging people's ages. I couldn't help but stare at her as she looked like she'd just stepped out of the pages of Vogue magazine. She had blue eyes, like the sky on the clearest day in summer, a perfect heart shaped face, long blonde hair, whiter than white teeth and she was wearing the most fabulicious white T-shirt and jeans with studs down the seams. I could tell that they cost mega bucks. *And she smells amazing*, I thought as her perfume wafted towards me on the breeze. It was sweet but delicate like the scent of white roses after the rain.

She handed me a piece of paper and said in an Essex accent, "I think this is yours darlin'."

I glanced down at it. Omigod! It was the same as the paper that had blown my way at school yesterday.

"Oh! But… this… I… er…" I began.

But the lady had already turned and was heading in the opposite direction. "Don't lose it this time," she called over her shoulder then gave me a wave as she walked away.

I looked at the paper again. *Weird*, I thought. *Why did she give it to me? Did she think I had dropped it?* Whatever the reason, it seemed like I really was meant to have it. This was the third time it had come to me. I decided to take a closer look later so stuffed it into my pocket and crossed the road to the shop.

As soon as I got inside, I started rummaging through the racks. There were a few things that looked promising and after fifteen minutes I had a bunch of outfits to try on. Even if they didn't fit perfectly, I could probably alter them as I'm good at adapting clothes. Art is one of the subjects that I come top in at school and being creative seems to come easy. Feeling more positive than I had all day, I went into the changing room.

The first outfit was a mid-length black dress in a floaty voile-type material. I slipped it over my head and looked in the mirror.

Waaaay too big. And the colour drained me. Even if I raced home and altered it on Mum's sewing machine, it wasn't going to work.

The second was a pink satin dress.

Bleurgh. I looked like a bridesmaid and the material was totally too shiny. Not flattering at all.

The third one was a pale mushroom colour but looked sophisticated.

Until I got it on that it is. It was waaaay too long. I looked like a kid in her mum's dress. And once again, the colour made me look washed out.

The fourth looked like it might be perfect. Short

with a halter neck line. Peacock blue. I read somewhere that it's a good colour for people with green eyes like me.

I held my breath and squeezed into it. Much too tight. Only a nine year-old would get into it.

Ah well, I thought as I reached for the fifth one, a white short lycra dress, *this looks like it might fit.*

It did. It was perfect. I did a twirl. And then I saw the back. It had a huge nasty stain like someone had split red wine down the back. No wonder its previous owner had given it away.

I felt so disappointed as I got dressed. Will's great idea wasn't going to work. I put the clothes back on the rail then had another rummage through but nothing, only way old-fashioned stuff that I wouldn't be seen dead in. I had picked all the best pieces out already.

I checked my watch. Two o'clock. The party started at six thirty and I still had nothing to wear but no way could I go in my tatty old clothes from last year. I'd have to think up some excuse to tell Georgie as to why I couldn't go.

I left the shop, crossed the road to the bus stop where I got out the leaflet I'd been given earlier. I took a closer look to try and fathom out why it had come to me. I scanned both sides. It advertised a deli. Yes, I could see that across the street. A beauty salon.

Pentangles. Yes, I could see that too. A cyber café. Hmm. Hadn't noticed that before. It also gave a website address for a site about astrology. I liked reading about stuff like that. All us Crazy Maisies did. We regularly read our horoscope in our girlie mags. Maybe my horoscope this month had something special to tell me. Maybe something about my predicament – a dance to go to but nothing to wear.

I decided that I'd take a look at the site when I got home if Dan and Will weren't hogging the computer, that is if it was even working, (it was an old one that Uncle Ernie had given us when he bought a new model for his own use. If it wasn't for him we'd be totally in the last century, because as well as donating the PC to us as a special Christmas present for all the family, he said he'd pay for our internet connection.)

Then I had a flash of inspiration. A cyber café was right opposite me. That meant computers. A computer that I could actually use without having to wait until the Brothers Grimm, Dan and Will, got off it. Bliss. And I could look up the astrology website right now and find out what my destiny for the month was.

I looked again at the cyber café. It was up at the end of the row and it looked like it was open as I could see people moving about inside. The shop front was painted in bright blue, silver and turquoise. I crossed the road and peered in the window. *Woah. Space age city,*

I thought as I took in the futuristic décor inside. The front half seemed to be a shop selling party stuff and novelty items but at the back, I could see several geeky-type people sitting at computers and at the very back was a counter selling drinks in bright fluorescent beakers. It looked like a cool place so I opened the door and ventured inside.

Gentle music floated out through loudspeakers in the corners. Choirs of angels singing. Looking around, I felt like I'd entered some kind of space ship. *Jeez*, I thought, *I've walked onto the set of a freaking Star Trek movie.* To the left of the door was a chrome counter behind which was the most extraordinary looking person. He had silver spiked-up hair and was dressed in an electric blue lycra jumpsuit and high silver platform boots. Very space age meets punk.

"Hey," he said as soon as he saw me. "Computers at the back. Use the one on the right."

"But…" I was about to ask how he knew that I wanted to use one of the computers but then rationalized that probably most people who went in there did so because like me, they hadn't ready access to one at home.

"Thanks," I said and made my way to the back of the shop.

I sat down in front of the screen and the space punk man came over and stood behind me. "Know how to use it?"

I glanced at the screen. "Think so."

"Internet you want, right?"

I nodded. "How much?"

"Free to you."

"Free?"

"Special promotion," he said as he leant over and moved the mouse so that the internet opened up. "Just type in the site you want."

"Thanks," I said.

"I'm Uri," he said. "Just give me a shout if you need anything." Then he winked and drifted off to help a new customer, a lady in her twenties, who had sat down a few feet away. I couldn't help but notice that when she asked how much to use the internet, Uri said, "pound an hour," and took her money! *Strange*, I thought, then decided that maybe it was a promotion for under fifteens or something.

I got the leaflet out, typed in the website address from the leaflet and waited for it to download. After a few moments, the screen appeared like a dark night sky. *Fitting for an astrology site*, I thought as soft tinkling music accompanied the picture unfolding.

A scroll floated down from the right hand corner of the screen and uncurled itself to reveal a form asking for my name, my date of birth, place of birth and time of birth. *Freaking fairy farts*, I thought. *I don't know the time I was born.* I got out my mobile and called Mum. Luckily she picked up.

"Hey, what time was I born, Mum?"

"Two fifteen in the morning," she said. "Why?"

"Tell you later," I said and hung up.

I typed in the time and sat back to wait for it to give me my horoscope. I liked being in the café. It had a tranquil atmosphere, like it was a space station hovering just outside earth. Everyone working away quietly. The angelic music playing out of the loudspeakers. Very peacefu...

Suddenly a trumpet fanfare *BLASTED* out of the computer. *Really LOUD.* I almost jumped out of my seat and so did a number of the computer geeks sitting nearby.

"Shhh," hushed one of them and gave me a filthy look.

"Not my fault," I whispered back. "*I* didn't know it was going to do that!"

But the noise was getting louder and louder.

"Congratulations," said a neon type message flashing on the screen. "You are this month's Zodiac Girl."

And the trumpet got even louder like the person playing it was bursting their cheeks and their lungs, liver and kidneys to hit the highest note.

I glanced around. Everyone in the café was staring

at me.

"Quiet," shushed another geek.

"Sorry," I called back to him. "It's one of those pop up things. I'll get rid of it."

Desperately, I scanned the keyboard for some kind of volume control. There it was up at the top. I pressed it as fast as I could but the music continued to get even louder. Everyone was still staring at me including Uri who was grinning his head off.

"Help," I mouthed to him.

He gave me the thumbs up and clapped his hands for attention. "Quiet everyone and let's hear it for this month's Zodiac Girl. Hip hip hoorah."

As he led the cheers, a few of the geeks looked at him as if he was mad.

"What are you doing?" I asked when he came over. "I don't want to disturb anyone any more than I already have. Please turn the noise off and get rid of that pop up thingy that's flashing. I can't get rid of it."

"But you're this month's Zodiac Girl," said Uri. "Why would you want to get rid of it? It's fantastic. Don't you realize what it means?"

"No I don't," I whispered. "Please, please turn the noise off. Everyone's staring."

Uri typed in a button and the sound went off. "There you are. So. How do you feel?"

"About what?"

"Being Zodiac Girl this month."

"Feel? Zodiac Girl? Nothing. I don't know what it means and anyway, isn't everyone who goes to this site a Zodiac Girl? It's some kind of promotion thing isn't it?"

"Heavens no. There's only one Zodiac Girl a month. Just you. And it means my dear," he said as he read the screen and saw my name, "that you, Tori have a *great* month ahead of you. Well hopefully great. It can go either way depending what you make of it. But all sorts of surprises in store. Hmm. Let me see. So your Sun is in Taurus? Taureans are ruled by Venus so that means you get Nessa as your guardian. Lucky you. She's faaaabulous. A goddess. You'll love her."

"Guardian? But… I don't want a guardian. I have a mum and a dad too although he doesn't live with us… what I mean to say is I don't need anyone to look after me so you can tell this Nessa that she won't be needed."

Uri laughed. "Tell her yourself. She'll be in touch, you can count on that."

I was starting to feel spooked. Like someone was following me. First the paper blowing at me in the school playground. Then the beautiful lady handing the *same* paper to me and now this. Fairies, angels or not, Megan could keep them. I got up to go. "Right.

Okay. Thanks. Got to go now."

Uri leant over to look at the screen. "You can ignore it if you want. Some do. Some people are afraid of the unknown and what they don't understand but…" he seemed to be scanning my birthchart. "No. Yours is not the chart of a coward."

Well I'm feeling decidedly cowardly now, I thought as I legged it to the door. As I opened it to leave, Uri called out, "There's a message on here for you, Zodiac Girl. Go back to where you have been and you will find what you seek."

"Right. Yes. Thank you. Bye," I stuttered as I shut the door behind me. Like, what in the world was that supposed to mean? Sometimes computer people could be way weird and this one took the biscuit. *I want to be home*, I thought. *Safe. Planet earth. Sofa. Telly. Normal.*

On the way back to the bus stop, I passed the charity shop again. As I glanced in the window, I noticed that the old lady in there was getting some things out of a bin-bag and hanging them on the rack behind the counter. One of the items caught my eye.

Short. Floaty voile material. Halter neck. With tiny weeny coral, primrose and black flowers. Really pretty.

I had to go back in.

"Excuse me," I said as I approached the lady behind the counter and pointed at the dress. "Er… is that for sale?"

She nodded and smiled. "It is. Looks like it's never been worn and it's just about your size too. It's just come in. Want to try it on?"

She handed me the dress and I took a quick glance at the label. Suzie Tsang. Omigod! I had read about her in one of the glossies last week. (Dan gets them for me. He does a paper round in a posh area and on recycling day, he looks through their magazine throw out bins and because he knows I like reading them, he brings me back all the copies of Vogue and Harpers.) So I knew Susie Tsang was only the hottest new designer in the country.

"Er... how much is it?" I asked the lady.

"How much for this, Dora?" the lady called to someone in a back room. She held up the dress.

"Not much fabric is there?" said a second white-haired lady appearing at the door. "Oh give us a pound for it if it fits you."

One pound for a Suzie Tsang dress! If only they knew. These dresses went for four or five hundred pounds in the shops in London. I couldn't believe my luck. A dress like that and I'd have change left over from the four pounds fifty I had in my purse!

Please, please, please let it fit, I begged the patron saint of charity shops as I went back into the changing room.

The angels, fairies, saints and leprechauns were

smiling upon me. The dress fitted like it had been specially made for me. It couldn't have looked more perfect. I could go to the ball and I didn't have to be a Nickynonames after all.

I got dressed, made my purchase and almost danced back to the bus stop. The sun was shining and I felt brilliant.

Only on the way bus did I remember the message for me that Uri had read from the astrology site. "Go back to where you have been and you will find what you seek."

Could it have meant go back to the shop? Go and buy the dress? Whatever. Yahey! Something was going my way. I had a great new dress. Maybe it was in the stars that things were looking up after all.

Chapter Four

Party time!

Back at home, I went into a frenzy of getting ready for the charity ball. I had a "steps to beauty" list that I'd cut out of my Star Girl magazine last year in case I ever got invited to an event like this but I never dreamt that it would happen so soon.

My list went:

Bathe: in my strawberry bubble bath that Mum got me for Christmas.

Exfoliate: with my mango scrub (pressie from Aunt Phoebe).

Moisturize: with apple body lotion.

Wash and condition my hair: with my blueberry shampoo and conditioner.

"Poo," said Dan when I came out the bathroom. "You smell like a fruit salad."

I didn't react. I was having fun and neither the fact that the boys had left water in the soap dish so that it was slimy, nor the fact that they'd left wet towels on the bathroom floor after their football practice, could ruin my mood. My world was good.

Next on the list were my nails and make-up. Mum normally doesn't let me wear make-up but as this was a special occasion, she allowed it and even lent me some of her rose-petal lipstick. While I was occupied beautifying myself, she was downstairs chatting to Aunt Pat and finishing off the cakes that she had made for the auction. Wonderful smells of baking and cinnamon and vanilla wafted up the stairs. As I got dressed and inhaled the gorgeous mixture of scents, a glow of happiness spread through me. It was going to be a good night. I could feel it in my bones.

By six thirty, I was dressed and ready to go. As I came down the stairs, I felt like I was in a movie. Even Andrea looked up from her book and raised her eyebrows when I went into the living room and did a Crazy Maisie model on the cat walk strut. Georgie, Megan, Hannah and I practised for hours in the school playground – hips thrust out, hand on hip, bottom lip out, cheeks sucked in.

"You look nice," she said. That is praise indeed coming from Andrea as she's not one to let much out about what's going on in her head.

Will gave a loud wolf whistle. "You look great," he said, "but cut the stupid walk."

"Yeah and the daft expression on your face. But you look good for a girl," said Dan then he looked out the window. "Your limo's here."

The boys helped Mum carry the cakes out and we all went out the front to get into the "limo".

Mum had talked Uncle Kev into giving us a lift up to the hotel in his white van because no way could Mum have carried the cakes on the bus and she wasn't going to cut into her profit by ordering a taxi. He was there on the dot and I got into the back with two of the cakes while Mum got in the front with another couple on her knee.

"Party time," I said with a grin as we chugged off. I could hardly wait to get there.

The atmosphere was buzzing when we reached the venue. Ladies in fabulous long evening gowns and men in black suits and bow ties were heading from their cars towards the steps of the hotel. BMWs, Mercedes, Range Rovers, a whole fleet of posh cars were already in the car park and as Uncle Kev drew up, I hoped that no-one was going to see me get out of the old van. I'd almost asked him to drop me on the corner before the hotel but I knew that I wouldn't have been able to walk the long drive in the shoes that I had borrowed from Mum. They were her best pair with kitten heels and pointy fronts (another charity shop find) plus Mum and Uncle Kev might have thought I was being sniffy about our ride and even though I was, I wouldn't have wanted to offend them.

"You go on in, poppet," said Mum when we stopped outside the kitchens round the back. "Go and find Georgie and I'll see you later."

I hopped out as quick as I could and raced round the front. It was a media frenzy as limos drove up, celebrities got out and flash bulbs went off as the paparazzi press called at them to look their way while they took photos. *Lucky it's a warm evening*, I thought, *so everyone really can show off their fab outfits and not have to hide them in coats.*

"Hey Tori," I heard a familiar voice call.

It was Georgie to my right. She looked mint in a soft blue mini dress and her hair up with little silver sparkles in it.

We did a quick *muwah*, *muwah*, kiss air to the left, kiss air to the right (the way posh ladies do when they meet up in town).

"You look amazing," I said as I stepped back.

"Thanks. You do too and wow, I so love your dress. Is it new?"

I nodded. "Yeah. Thanks. It's a Suzie Tsang. Mum got it for me on her last trip to London."

"Suzie Tsang? Omigod. I love her stuff. It must have cost a fortune."

"You'd be shocked if you knew," I said and gave her my best modest look.

All further talk about our outfits was cut short as another limo drew up and the photographers went ballistic.

"Oh wow!" said Georgie. "Look. It's Marsha Johnson off the telly!"

Whoever said that money can't buy happiness? They had clearly never been to an event like this, I thought as we stood and watched famous guest after famous guest arrive, smile for the cameras, then go inside. I couldn't believe that I was really going to be in there with them but yes, we showed our tickets to the security man on the steps and he waved us through with the rest of them.

Freaking awesome, I thought as we stepped inside the vast reception hall. There was so much to look at and take in. Flower arrangements as big as a bus. Marble pillars that looked the real thing, not that fake plastic sort you can buy at DIY stores. Glittering chandeliers with a million candle bulbs shimmering light. So many people all dressed in their best outfits, the sound of chattering, laughing, champagne bottles popping, glasses chinking. Georgie and I had a great time watching and gossiping about the ones who had no dress sense and drooling over those who'd got it right. In the main ballroom, disco music was playing and strobe lights flashing and already a few people were up dancing. In another small hall, we could see that there were tables groaning with food and at the back was a small stage where I spotted Mum laying out her cakes.

"Shall we go and get something?" asked Georgie as she peeked in. "I'm starving."

I quickly steered her away. I didn't want her to know that Mum was working in there and was not a guest.

"I'll go and get us a drink and something to nibble on," I said. "I'll bring it to you in the dance room. You go and check out if there are any cute boys in there."

"Good plan," said Georgie, and disappeared off into the disco.

As I went in to get the drinks, Mum spotted me and I gave her a wave but didn't go over, she looked busy anyhow. As I got the drinks, I noticed Sonia Marks and Chloe Philips from Year Nine at the other end of the table. Sonia pointed at me then put her hand to her friend's ear and whispered something. Chloe whipped around and stared at me and then they both started laughing. Whatever they'd said wasn't nice. I could tell. *Maybe they know that my mum is part of the staff and I don't really belong here*, I thought and turned my back on them quickly.

On the way back through the disco, I noticed everyone turn to look at someone who had just arrived. Thinking that it must be another celebrity, I turned to look as well. For a moment, I was blinded as flash bulb after flash bulb blasted off. When my eyes adjusted, I saw that it was a couple who had arrived. *Freaking bejeezjobs, do they look the bis boz*, I thought as I stared along with others gaping at them, *pure gossip magazine material*. The lady looked familiar. As my eyes focused properly, I realized that it was the beautiful lady who had given me the leaflet this morning in Osbury! She was on the arm of a man who looked like he'd just walked off a film set in Hollywood. She looked like a goddess dressed in an off the shoulder, long, Grecian-style, ivory dress, her hair was up and she was wearing silver star earrings. And he looked like a God. Tall, handsome, suntanned with a mane of shoulder length black wavy hair and with the same whiter-than-white teeth that the lady had. They radiated the X factor like they ate charisma flakes for breakfast. Everyone was staring at them, both men and women alike. The lady looked around the room and waved at someone in my direction.

I turned to see who but there was no-one behind me. She waved again. Omigod. Was she waving at *me*? She couldn't be. But she was. She was even coming over!

She stopped in front of me and smiled. "Hey Tori," she said. "It is Tori, innit? I thought I might see you 'ere. I'm Nessa."

I was so gobsmacked I stood there doing my

goldfish impression. Why was she talking to me? Everyone was watching. But Nessa, *Nessa*? I had heard that name somewhere and I recognized the scent, white roses and rain. Where? *Where*? I urged my brain to get into gear. Oh yes. Nessa. It was the name of the person that the Captain of the Space Age Nutters' shop, Uri, had said was to be my guardian. He *couldn't* have meant this lady could he? No way. She looked like a famous person. Footballer's wife famous. And not mad the way Uri looked. And *certainly* not some sad teenager's guardian.

When I finally got my bottom lip up off the floor and got my mouth to work, I said, "Hi. Um. Yes. I'm Tori."

"My Zodiac Girl," she said with a smile. "Tori Taylor. Taurus. I saw your chart."

With the excitement of coming to the dance, until now, I'd forgotten about the strange announcement from the computer this afternoon. I certainly didn't think I'd hear any more about it as I thought it was some computer pop up thing that displayed when anybody went to the astrology site that I'd typed in. No big deal. But hey, if it meant that this amazing woman was going to talk to me, I didn't mind. People were still watching us. *Famous by association. I can do that,* I thought as I shifted about on my feet and tried to look cool. People were actually looking at me as if I might be somebody.

"Yes, um, that's me, Zodiac Girl," I said and gave her a smile. "Tori is short for Victoria. All my friends call me that. Tori that is, not Victoria."

"Then I shall," said Nessa, "because I 'ope that we will be mates."

Mates with someone like her! That would be awesome, I thought, so I gave her what I hoped was my most winning smile.

Before we could talk any more, an old man with a white beard appeared, gave me what I can only describe as a "what kind of hole did you crawl out of?" look and pulled her away so that I didn't have a chance to ask her anything more about Zodiac Girls or guardians.

The rest of the evening went by in a blur. Cute waiters brought round trays of canapés and drinks, and Georgie and I stuffed our faces on the sweet ones. They were way tasty: mini chocolate cakes with raspberry sauce, teeny-weeny lime cheesecakes and itsy bitsy pancakes with maple syrup. Yumbolicious. After the nibbles, we had such a laugh in the disco. We went through the repertoire of dances that we had practised on various sleepovers with Meg and Hannah. Our range went from Russian Cossack dancing (which I was rubbish at because I kept falling over when we had to do the balance on one leg while kicking out with the other bit) to Spanish to Egyptian to cowboy line dancing to ballet to Riverdancing. I think some people thought that we were totally mad but we didn't care. We were having such a good time and a cute-looking boy with dark floppy hair even asked me to dance with him and joined in with gusto as we did our "dances from around the globe". *This is the life for me*, I thought as we did the Highland Fling around the dance floor. *I was born for the high life*.

Towards the end of the evening, we drifted out into an adjacent hall where the handsome man who had arrived with Nessa was introduced as Mr Sonny Olympus, otherwise known as Mr O. He got up to start an auction and I could see people nudging each other and whispering as the bidding got underway. I could see immediately that it wasn't in a nasty way like Chloe and Sonia from our school had been about me. I could see it was in admiration.

Mr O was brilliant and whipped up people's enthusiasm so that they were really going for it in attempts to outbid each other.

"And what am I bid for this fabulous hamper from Brecknams and Stasons?" he asked in the kind of voice that sounded like one of those men who do the chocolate commercials on telly. Deep and velvety. "Let's start the bidding at one hundred pounds."

"Five million squillion," I said and pretended to put my hand up but Georgie laughed and pushed it down.

"Two hundred," called a voice from the back.

And up and up it went until it reached two thousand! I did a quick calculation in my head. *That much money would feed our whole family for a year I bet. There must be some stonkingly-rich people here*, I thought, although looking around, I reckoned that most of them just wanted to impress Mr O and get his attention, especially the women.

The auction continued with people outbidding each other for all sorts of rubbish. A bottle of old wine went for two hundred and fifty pounds. *Mad*, I thought, *especially when you could buy a brand new one for around six pounds.*

"Just who is Mr O?" asked Georgie.

"He's an actor," I said in a deep actor like voice. "I overheard someone saying that anyway."

"Thought so," she replied.

Next up were Mum's cakes and when she took them up on the stage, I noticed that Mr Olympus made a great fuss of her. She even blushed. I could see her cheeks flush from half way down the hall. I felt pleased to see her looking like she was enjoying herself and she looked pretty tonight in a red dress that Aunt Pat had lent her.

With Mr O's help, the cakes were a huge hit and

raised over a hundred pounds each. I felt so proud of her and nudged Georgie.

"My mum made those," I said.

"Yeah, my mum does a lot of work for charity too," she replied.

I didn't tell her that Mum had been paid to make the cakes. It was Mrs Jackson that actually donated them. Donating to charity was a luxury that our family couldn't afford at the moment.

"And now for the raffle," Mr O announced when the last item for auction had gone.

A fat bald man got up to join him on stage and held out a sack.

Mr Olympus put his hand in and pulled out a ticket. "And the winner of the picnic hamper is number one hundred and forty four."

"That's me!" cried a lady with frizzy red hair at the front who made her way to the stage where she was presented with her prize.

A few other people had their ticket numbers called and they too went to collect their prizes.

"Let's go and get a drink," I said to Georgie and we turned to go out of the auction room.

"And finally," said Mr Olympus as he put his hand in the sack and pulled out a ticket, "the last prize. And the winner is… number twelve… and the ticket belongs to… Tori Taylor."

"Omigod," said Georgie pulling me back. "That's you! I never saw you buy a ticket."

"I… I didn't," I said as she shoved me forward. *I haven't got one. Maybe Mum had got one for me*, I thought as I made my way up to the stage.

Up on the stage, Mr O gave me a parcel. As I took it, he gave me a wink.

"But I don't have the ticket," I said.

"No matter," he said. "The parcel has got your name on it. Tori Taylor?"

I wasn't going to argue. "Right. Wow, thanks," I said and raced back to join Georgie and unwrap it.

We ripped off the wrapping paper and inside was the coolest mobile phone I had ever seen. It was so pretty, tiny, in a pale pearly green with a glittering jewel the colour of an emerald set in it. I immediately put it up to my ear and did the Crazy Maisie cat-walk strut out into the corridor and back.

"Wow," said Georgie. "That is the cutest phone I have ever seen. It's like it was made for a fairy princess or something. I wonder where it came from, I've certainly never seen one like it in any of the shops. Oh and look, there's something else."

At the bottom of the parcel was a small box. I opened it to find a silver chain with a charm of some sort on it. When I looked closer, I saw that it was the zodiac sign for Taurus. *This night is just getting better and better*, I thought as I fastened the chain around my neck.

Just at that moment, Sonia and Chloe passed by and Sonia bumped into me.

"Sorr*eeee*," she said in a false way. "Wasn't looking where I was going."

I was sure that she'd done it on purpose.

Chloe looked me up and down. "Hi Nicky," she said then sniggered.

I felt a rush of panic. "I… My name is Tori actually," I said.

"Yeah right," said Sonia then leant forward and whispered in my ear. "But you're still a Nickynonames…"

I felt my stomach tighten and my face flush red. *Oh God no*, I thought. *Could she possibly know that I'd got my dress from the second-hand shop?*

"What's your problem?" said Georgie coming to my defence.

"Just ignore them," I said and began to pull her away. "It's nothing."

"Didn't you tell your friend then?" said Sonia.

"Tell me what?" asked Georgie squaring up to her.

"That your mate here is a Nickynonames," said Chloe.

"Don't you call her that," said Georgie.

"Why not? She is one. Your mate here can't afford

to buy designer gear unless she buys it in charity shops."

"Er, excuse me. She's only wearing a Susie Tsang," said Georgie. "You don't see too many of *those* in charity shops now do you?"

Inwardly I felt as if I was dying. This *couldn't* be happening.

Chloe burst out laughing. "No. You don't unless you go to Osbury. See, that dress used to belong to Sonia. She gave it to a charity shop earlier today, didn't you Sonia?"

Sonia nodded.

"There are more places than charity shops to buy dresses you know," said Georgie. "Tell her Tori. Tell her that your mum got it for you in London."

"I... I..." I had no excuse and felt exposed and near to tears. "I..."

"You said it's a Susie Tsang dress right?" said Sonia.

I didn't say anything.

"Yeah," said Georgie. "So, what are you trying to say, Sonia?"

"So, Susie Tsang is my aunt and she made it for me specially for my fifteenth birthday and your friend couldn't have bought it in London because she only made one and that was for me. So there."

"Well maybe she liked it so much, she made two or even three," said Georgie. "Go on *tell* her Tori."

But I still couldn't speak. I felt frozen from my toes to my tongue. Like someone had sprayed me with instant ice.

Sonia leant over and pulled the back of the neck of my dress up. "Here," she said. "Look at the label. The handstitched label. It says, 'For Sonia.'"

"So why did you give it away?" asked Georgie who looked like she'd like to hit Sonia.

Sonia feigned a yawn. "Oh you know. I've worn it a few times now so I'm bored with it. I don't really like wearing things that people have seen me in before. So passé, don't you think, to wear the same things over and over? And Aunt Susie's made me so many things over the years. I gave it to my mum to give to charity."

"So that some *poor* unfortunate could wear it but I bet you never expected to see it turn up here, hey Sonia?" added Chloe.

By now I felt my face was crimson. I felt that everyone in close proximity had heard what the girls were saying and was staring at me. I wanted the ground to open up and swallow me.

Sonia started singing in a slow mocking voice, "Nickynonames, nickynoooonames, nickynonaaaaaames..."

Chloe joined in with her. "Nickynonames, nickynoooonames, nickynonaaaaaames..."

I felt so ashamed. Everyone *was* looking. Suddenly

my great night, my dream-come-true, had turned into my worst nightmare. I felt like I was on stage with nothing on and everyone watching, waiting to see what I was going to do. I didn't dare look Georgie in the face. I'd lied to her so I knew she'd be looking at me and hating me.

I turned on my heel and fled.

Chapter Five

Old mate, new mate

I ran straight into the nearest Ladies, found a cubicle and locked the door. I felt so humiliated. I was sure all the people around had heard. Nickynonames. That was me. The discount diva. Silly little poor girl trying to act like she belonged when everyone could see that she was wearing someone's throw-outs. Stupid, sad, pathetic me. I felt so numb with shock that I couldn't even cry. I could hardly breathe either. It felt like someone had put a rope around my chest and pulled it tight. And then I felt a wave of anger. Zodiac Girl. Freaking Zodiac Girl. It was that stupid nutter at the cyber café who had caused this mess – with his "go back and you will find what you seek" rubbish. If it wasn't for that leaflet and that astrology site and that message and that dress, I wouldn't be the biggest *loser* in history hiding in a loo while everyone outside gossips about what a pathetic sad reject I am.

I kicked the cubicle door. "*Eeeeooooow!*" I cried as I stubbed my toe on the hard wood. I hopped around in the tiny space. It really hurt, like I'd dipped it in fire.

I have to get out of here without anyone seeing me, I thought. *But how? And where could I go?* I wanted to go some place and hide. But not home. There was no privacy there. Everyone would want to know how the evening went. I couldn't even hide in my bedroom because I shared it with Andrea and I could hardly shut her out. *Fairy farts*, I thought. *Freaking fairy farts. There was only one thing for it. I'd have to run away. Take to the road and go somewhere where no-one knows me. Maybe to London or one of the big cities. But I'd have no money. And I'd be hungry and have nowhere to sleep except a park bench under a bit of old newspaper. And I'd have no friends. And no Mum or Auntie Pat or Phoebe. And no Marmite or Meatloaf to cuddle up to. I'd even miss Dan and Will and Andrea. I'd fade away until someone would find my poor starved body underneath a bridge and they'd bring me back here and bury me and everyone I know would come to my funeral and cry buckets. Even those horrible girls Chloe and Sonia would come and see what happened and realize that they were to blame and they'd feel responsible as my coffin was lowered into the grave...*

As I was sitting there feeling very sorry for myself, I heard the sound of ringing. It was coming from my bag. I looked inside. It was my new mobile phone. *But I haven't given anyone the number yet*, I thought. *I don't even know it myself!*

Tentatively, I answered the call.

"Tori, it's Nessa. Where are you?" said a voice at the other end.

Oh please don't let her have seen what happened too, I thought. "Nowhere," I said.

"Nowhere. Now that's clever," said Nessa. "I've never been there myself. What's it like?"

I almost laughed but then I remembered that my life was over and I was miserable. "It's… okay, I'm not really nowhere."

"You sound upset. What's the matter darlin'?"

"Nothing."

"Ah nothing. That always upsets me n'all."

This time I did laugh.

"That's better," said Nessa.

"Sorry," I said. "Just I'm not feeling myself…"

"Then who are you feelin'?" asked Nessa.

"No-one. I mean I'm feeling a little mad tonight…"

"Ah that'll be 'cause of the moon. Where the moon is placed in your chart can make everyone feel a little bonkers some days. Listen Tori, I've been lookin' at your chart. Do you know much 'bout astrology?"

"Yes. No. At least I know a little. I know there are twelve signs and that I'm Taurus and that's the sign of the bull."

"That's right. There are twelve signs. They're called Sun signs. For you as a Taurus that means the Sun was in the sign of Taurus when you were born. April the twenty first to May the twenty first. Anyone born under those dates will be Taurus. Did you know though that there are lots of other planets that influence your chart?"

"No."

"Well there are. Ten of them. The Sun, the Moon, Jupiter, Mars, Venus, Saturn, Pluto, Uranus, Mercury and Neptune."

"Oh really?" I said trying to sound interested although I wondered why on earth she had picked this moment in time to give me a lecture in astrology. "How fascinating."

"Yeah, it is," continued Nessa. "And for you, Saturn and Pluto are squared to your moon at the moment."

"Sounds painful," I joked.

"Too right. No laughin' matter," said Nessa, "'cause what it means is that life is teaching you a serious lesson."

"Oh. What's that then?"

"Only you can know that Tori. I'm just 'ere to guide and advise but Saturn is sometimes known as the task master. In plain English, that means 'e can be a miserable bugger at times but you should listen to what 'e 'as to say to you. He does talk sense. Pluto is the planet of transformation and the Moon governs the psyche, feelin's, all that kinda stuff. Get those three planets squared up to each other in a chart like they are in yours right now, and it can mean an emotional ride. As a Taurean, I'm your guardian and I'm takin' special care of you this month so call me from your new phone if you need or want to ask anythin'. Think of me as a new mate. Okay?"

"Um. Okay," I said although I couldn't help think, *how weird is this? What is she on about? In fact, maybe I shouldn't be talking to her at all. Mum always told us not to talk to strangers and I don't really know anything about her. She maybe beautiful but that doesn't mean she's not bananarama and come to think of it… how did she get my phone number?*

"Er Nessa, how did you know this number?"

"Because you're Zodiac Girl this month, right? All Zodiac Girls get a phone like that – well, similar anyway. We try to make them in the colour right for your birth sign. The phone came from me. It's so you can get in touch with me, your guardian or any of the other planets for that matter. We've all got your new number."

"We?" I asked. I was starting to feel uncomfortable. "And who would the we be?"

"I told you, me and the other planets. Remember?"

"*Other* planets? Okaaaay…" I asked as all my alarm bells went off.

"Yes," said Nessa. "I told you there are nine others. Planets that is. You met one of them. The Sun, aka

Sonny Olympus, he's 'ere tonight. He led the auction right?"

"Right," I said although I was thinking, *wroooong*.

"And then there's Mars, the Moon, Jupiter, Pluto, Saturn, Uranus – you met him, Uri, 'e runs the Cyber café and Mercury, 'e's around somewhere too. You'll like 'im. All the girls do though I don't think there are any major encounters with 'im this month, least not from looking at your chart. You might see 'im in passing though. We call 'im Hermie. Anyway to cut a long story short, we're all 'ere on earth in human form."

Woah!!! I thought. *This lady is not only bananarama. She's the whole freaking fruit bowl. Best humour her and then avoid her like the plague.*

"Oh yes. Absolutely. Of course. And you are?"

"Nessa aka Venus. Venus rules Taurus which is why I'm your guardian for the month."

Omigod! She thinks she's a planet! Like how severely delusional can you get? I had heard of people thinking that they were Napoleon or Cleopatra or teapots but I had never heard of anyone thinking that they were a *planet* before, never mind Venus specifically.

"Guardian. Um. Yes. Er… That's what your (*fellow nutter*, I thought) friend Uri said as well."

"Right," said Nessa, "but I hope we can be mates too because mates are important right? More important than most things. So come out of your 'iding place in nowhere-land and don't be afraid. Not everything is as it seems."

"Yes. Course not," I said. "Actually I'm feeling fine now. Thanks for the chat. Yes. Better be getting along. Er… okay. Got to go now. Things to do. People to see."

"Tori, you sound strange. Are you sure you're okay duck?" asked Nessa.

"Oh yes. Tip top. Tippety top in fact. No need to worry about me. All better now. Thanks. Goodbye." *And don't forget to take your medication*, I thought as I heard the door to the Ladies open and close.

"Call me if you need."

"Okee dokee. Will do," I whispered. *Not a chance*, I thought but I didn't want to upset her or alert her to the fact that I knew she was a few stars short of a constellation. I also wanted to get her off the phone as I didn't want whoever had come in to the Ladies to think I was the mad one and talking to myself. Luckily Nessa had finished whatever she had to say for the time being and said "bye then," and hung up.

I clicked the phone shut, held my breath and drew my feet up from the floor so that whoever it was wouldn't know that I was in there. A moment later, the door opened again and someone had burst in.

"You *total mingers*," said a voice that I recognized as

Georgie's. "That was *way* out of order. Way cruel. So my mate bought your dress. So what? It looks great on her. That's what counts."

The knot in my stomach tightened.

"But you have to admit," said a voice that I also recognized as Sonia's, "it was funny wasn't it, Chloe? Her face went scarlet."

"Purple, I'd say," sniggered her friend.

"And you find *that* entertaining?" asked Georgie. "Ruining someone's night? You sad, pathetic sickos. This is supposed to be a charity ball, you know. Where's your spirit of sharing then? Huh? Where? I think you two are possibly the meanest people that I have ever met and I hope something really rotten happens to you."

"Oo-er, get her," sneered Sonia.

"Have you ever heard of karma?" Georgie continued. "Probably not because you're probably both as stupid as you are horrible. Well *I* know what it is. It means that your actions bring results and if you are mean to people, it will come back on you. If not in this lifetime then in the next. You will probably come back as the lowest of the low. As frog spawn."

The girls started laughing. "Frog spawn? Yeah right."

"Actually no, not frog spawn because frogs are nice. No, You'll come back as flies. Flies that eat poo."

I almost started laughing in my hiding place. *Good one Georgie*, I thought.

"Oh let's go, Chloe," said Sonia. "I'm bored with this silly little girl."

"Yes, not my first choice of company either," said Chloe.

I heard the door open and shut again and waited to see if they had gone out.

"Good riddance," I heard Georgie say. There was silence then she asked, "Tori, is that you in there?"

I held my breath.

"I know you're in there," she said. "I can hear you breathing."

And then I heard a scuffling and her face appeared at the gap at the bottom of the door. "And I can see you."

"It's not me," I said then realized that was totally stupid.

We both burst out laughing.

"Idiot," said Georgie. "I can see that it's you."

"I know. I… I'm sorry. I'm sorry I lied. I'll do anything to make it up to you. Be your slave for the rest of eternity…"

"Oh for heaven's sake Tori. Come out of there. I don't care where you got the dress from…"

I lowered my feet back down to the floor, got up, unlocked the cubicle and went out to join her. "Don't you?" I asked. "See, I did lie to you. I did get the dress from a charity shop and I should have told you the truth but... I thought you'd hate me."

"No way. You're my mate. I understand. Well. Sort of."

"I went to Osbury to look for a dress and there this was in the charity shop window and it looked so fab and..."

"You don't have to explain, Tori. I got something from a charity shop once too. A Monopoly game. Why not? Just don't lie to me again."

I still felt bad. Ashamed. "I think I ought to go home now."

Georgie looked appalled. She put one hand on her hip and wagged a finger at me with the other hand. "Tori Taylor, we are at one of the *bestest* parties we've ever been invited to and you want to go home and leave me on my own! No way. Now that *would* upset me. Just now you said you were sorry and that you wanted to make it up to me for lying. Okay. Here's your chance. Stay."

"But what if *everyone* knows that my dress is second hand?"

"*Tooori*," said Georgie in an exasperated voice. "The universe does *not* revolve around you. Probably no-one even noticed the two ugly sisters having a go at you just now. And anyway, I bet you anything most of the people here have hired their outfits and that's no different to wearing something second-hand is it?"

"I guess," I said.

"And most of them are more concerned about what *they* look like and having a good time than where some teenage girl got her dress from…"

"Suppose."

"So let's go."

She opened the Ladies door for me, tucked her hand through my arm and shoved me out.

"Bossy boots," I said but I squeezed her arm as I said it and she gave me a big smile back. She was a good mate. I hadn't realized until that night just how good, but here she was sticking up for me and talking me out of my misery. *Phew*, I thought, *maybe I don't have to run away after all. That's a relief.* I so wasn't ready to do starvation, loneliness and homelessness.

As we made our way back into the party, I saw that Georgie was right. No-one was the slightest bit interested in me or what I was up to. They were all too busy enjoying the fun. Suddenly it didn't matter that my dress was second-hand. I had one of the best friends in the world and the evening wasn't over yet.

As we made our way down the corridor, I spotted Mr O chatting to the mayor and then checking his appearance and smoothing his hair down in a mirror.

I nudged Georgie to look.

"Bit of a luvvie, don't you think?" she remarked.

"Bit of a loves himself by the look of it," I said. "I reckon that he'd be a heart throb for the older ladies though, don't you think?"

"I guess," said Georgie.

"Hold on a sec. I just want to ask him something," I said. *If Mr O knows the mayor, I thought, and he runs the auction then he must be on the level. And he might be able to shed some light on whether Nessa is totally nuts-in-May or not.*

"Okay, I'll see you in the disco then?" said Georgie and took off in the direction of the dance hall.

"Okay," I called after her and went over to Mr O. "Excuse me sir, but…"

"Ah Zodiac Girl," he said. "Call me Sonny. So how goes it in the land of Taurus?"

"Um… good I guess. About this Zodiac thing. I wanted to ask you if you know what it's all about. I mean, where did that phone you gave me come from and who's that lady you came with?

His face lit up with a dazzling smile. "Ah. Questions, questions," he said then he looked me up and down, put his hands on my shoulders, pushed them back then stepped behind me and thumped in the middle of my back. "First girl, look to your posture. Most important thing they teach at acting school. Stand up straight. Come on. Walk tall. Chin up."

He was so commanding that I found myself doing as he asked.

"Good girl," he said and then began doing the look-up-and-down thing again. "Hhm, yes. Nice dress, Tori. Suits you. Always remember with clothes, it's the way you wear them. A girl can be dressed in designer labels but look like nothing. Another can be dressed in old cast-offs and look like a million dollars. All down to posture and confidence."

Oh no, I thought as I felt my face blush scarlet. *Georgie was wrong. Everyone in the place did know I was wearing second-hand clothes.* "So you know about my dress then?"

"Know what?" he asked.

"That it's second-hand."

"Second-hand? Is it? Marvellous. Good for you. You've clearly got a good eye. I love a bargain myself. And it's the right dress for you. What does it matter if it's second-hand?"

"I… I guess it doesn't…"

"See here Tori, Nessa showed me your chart. Lacking in self-esteem, it said. Needs to value herself more. You need to work on that which is why I say, chin up, shoulders back, walk tall."

I laughed. "Bossy, aren't you?"

He looked offended. "I just know what works. So you were asking about the lady I came with?"

"Yes. Is she... er...?" I was about to say, "Is she all right in the head?" but then thought he might be offended if she was his date.

"She's a goddess," he said. "A darling. You're lucky to have her as your guardian."

"Guardian. What exactly does that mean?"

"You're Zodiac Girl, aren't you?"

I nodded. "I guess."

"So Nessa's yours for a month. Someone to turn to sort of thing. Nothing weird in case you're worried. Now would you care to dance?"

"Dance? Me? Oh I can't..."

"No such word as can't..." said Mr O as he proffered me his arm. "Hey, there's the cake maker extraordinaire."

I glanced up and saw Mum about to go into the Ladies. She turned and waved when she saw us.

"Mum," I called. "This is Mr Olympus, Mr O, I mean Sonny. He's asked me to dance."

Mum blushed. "Oh I know who he is," she said. "We met earlier. Go ahead, Tori. I'll catch up with Georgie and we'll come and watch."

Mr O took my hand, tucked it into his arm and we made our way into the dance hall. Once again, I felt people staring but this time, it was with curiosity and envy. Sonny was easily the best-looking man in the room even if he was old enough to be my dad. I spotted Sonia and Chloe at the drinks table and gave them a casual wave. Their jaws dropped open. They so didn't expect to see me back at the party. Georgie was dancing on the other side of the hall and gave me the thumbs up when she saw me.

"Okay, young Zodiac thing," said Sonny as we began to move to the music, "now, shoulders back and dazzle, darling, dazzle."

We fell into a dance routine as if we'd been rehearsing for days. Soon a crowd gathered around us and began to clap. It was like Mr O was totally tuned into me and what move I was going to make next. To the left we stepped, then to the right in perfect time with one another.

Suddenly Mr O grabbed a rose from a nearby table, held it with his teeth and began to clap. I got the message and we went into a bit of spontaneous mad flamenco.

"Ole, ole, ole, ole," said Mr O through his teeth while I danced around him Spanish style and onlookers cheered. When we'd finished, we both burst out laughing and he gave me a hug.

"Laugh and the world laughs with you, cry…" Mr O started to say.

"And you cry alone," I finished for him and gave him a big smile.

"Well done, Zodiac Girl," he said.

An astonished Chloe and Sonia watched from the side and I could see the envy in their eyes. They probably imagined I'd be blubbing in a corner somewhere because of them. *Well I'm not,* I thought, *you don't get rid of me that easily!*

Chapter Six

Miniature people

"That's *so* cool," said Megan after I'd shown her and Hannah my new phone while we were on the bus going to school on Monday morning. Both of them were well impressed but I still wasn't sure that I wasn't being pursued by the local nut jobs. Nessa had sent a text before breakfast. "Cm to Osbry 1 nght aftr skl, Nessa ***" it said. I noted the star symbols instead of kisses.

Yeah right, I thought. *Except she might have some creepy-crawly hitman waiting there to kidnap me and sell me to the slave trade in some intergalactic universe deep in space. It happens all the time on the telly.*

I didn't really know what to think about the whole Zodiac thing even though Mr O had said that Nessa was okay. I wanted to believe him but then he might be King of the Bongo Beings and she his queen for all I knew. In the cold light of Sunday morning, I had thought it all over and decided that the whole deal sounded unreal. The whole evening had been extrordinary and I hadn't exactly been my normal self either. But stars, planets, zodiacs? No thanks, way too out there for me. But the phone I'd been given was so cute that I couldn't resist taking it into school. Georgie had said that she'd never seen one like it. It would be my chance to show something off for a change. Not that it worked very well as a phone. I had tried typing all my mate's numbers into it but it wouldn't take them. And it already had the names of a load of people I didn't know listed in the directory.

Hannah and Meg were dying to hear all about the dance on Saturday. I filled them in on most of it (not the bit about the dress though – I'd had to eat enough humble pie for one week) and told them all about the Zodiac thing and how I'd been given the phone and the necklace.

"Wow, I wish I was a Zodiac Girl," said Megan. "It sounds great. Maybe we can try the site at lunch-time in the library and see if I'm one too."

"We can," I said, "but from what I could make out from the guy who runs the cyber café, there is only one a month. And I don't think everyone gets to be a Zodiac Girl."

"So what makes you one then?" asked Megan.

"I don't know. I haven't really had a chance to ask much about it. Nessa, she's the lady I told you about who said that she's my guardian, she said something about there being ten planets all here in human form. But don't you think that sounds mad? I mean, they might be a bunch of loony petunies for all I know…"

"Nah," said Megan. "I don't think it sounds that weird. It's not like they've asked you to do anything dodgy like get into a car with them or lured you to an isolated spot. You're not stupid. You know the rules about strangers and what have they done? They've given you pressies. I think they sound like angels or fairies."

I should have known that she'd react like that.

"Give us another look at the phone then," said Hannah.

I passed her the phone and she and Meg were well impressed.

"Brill, it's a camera phone," said Megan and she held it up to take some pictures. "Least I think it is…"

I hadn't realized that it could take pics as I'm not as techno-savvy as her and Hannah.

"Really?" I said. "Let's see."

But Hannah was busy with it. "I can't get it to take pics but oh look," she said as she pressed a button. "There are already some shots on here. Wow. Who are this lot?"

The three of us leant in so that we could all see.

"And there's a text waiting for you," said Megan

who pressed another button then began to read. "Hi. You seemed unsure about everything on Saturday. Here are the guys I told you about. Hope we can be of some help in your month as Zodiac Girl, Nessa, kiss, kiss, although she's put stars not crosses. Wow. It's as if she read your mind and knew that you were worried."

"Or maybe she's done this before and coaxed innocent young girls..." I began.

"Oh chill out, Tori," said Hannah. "You watch too many horror films. Let's have a look at what's on there."

We leant in again. Megan pressed a button and a video film began to play on the tiny screen. First there was a shot of Nessa with a big smile on her face, standing in what looked like a florist shop as there were huge vases of flowers all around her. She held up her hands and tiny pale pink heart shaped flowers began to fall like cherry blossom in spring.

"Wow. She's really beautiful," said Megan. "Like a fairy princess."

"And look," said Hannah, "the flowers are forming words on the wooden floor in front of her. What are they saying?"

"Nessa for Venus," I read.

"That's so pretty," said Megan, "and look here comes another one."

This time, it was Mr O who stepped into the screen. He was dressed in white and was in a field of bright yellow sunflowers.

Megan did a wolf whistle causing a few people on the bus to turn around and stare at us.

"He's so handsome," said Hannah. "That has to be your Mr O right?"

I nodded.

"I think I've seen him in a movie," Hannah continued, "and look, the sunflower petals are also making words, Sonny for the sun. Wow! Like how have they done that?"

Megan put her hand on her heart. "Magic," she sighed. "I knew it existed. I just knew it."

"Oh get real, dozo," I said. "It's *technology*. They can do anything with it these days for business promotions, advertising or whatever. I mean, look at the Harry Potter movies. You don't really think that Hagrid the giant is really that size, do you?"

Megan stuck her tongue out at me.

"Don't like the look of this one," said Hannah as the screen dimmed and the city scene was replaced by the interior of a classroom with a blackboard. A very stern-looking man with white hair and a beard at a desk came into view. He peered over his glasses at us and looked like he was very annoyed to be there. He stood up and wrote in squeaky chalk on the blackboard: Dr Cronus. Saturn. Then he stomped off.

"He was at the ball on Saturday," I said. "He spoke to Nessa at one point. In fact, she said something to me about Saturn. Something about him being the one that teaches lessons or something."

Megan shivered. "He looks very strict," she said. "I wouldn't want him as my guardian. What sign does Saturn rule?"

"Don't know," I replied.

"You could ask Nessa afterwards," said Megan. "She's bound to know."

The scene on the phone screen was changing again. This time it was to a dark basement with deep, wine-red walls, burgundy, velvet drapes and lit candles in a huge silver candelabra around what looked like a long wooden coffee table.

"Bit spooky," said Hannah.

"I like it," said Megan. "Very Goth chic. Omigod, the table's a *coffin*!"

"And it's *opening*!" cried Megan. "I don't like it!"

The coffin was indeed opening. Someone was in there! And whoever it was, was coming out! A man. First he sat up then stood and stepped out of the coffin. He looked middle-aged with a dark ponytail and was wearing a dark velvet suit and had a burgundy scarf (that matched the drapes) around his neck.

"Matching accessories. Cool," I commented.

Megan had her hands over her eyes. "Can't look, can't look," she said.

"It's a man, Meg" I said as I watched the screen. "He looks okay. Not scary."

He wasn't spooky dooky looking at all and soon Megan was watching with Hannah and I again. He had a long face and a big nose and there was something about him that looked interesting, like you could have a jolly good conversation with him about all sorts of things. He held out a fisted hand then opened it to show that there on his palm was a caterpillar. The man blew on it and it became a chrysalis and then a butterfly. He gave a deep bow and from behind him and behind the drapes came hundreds of butterflies flying round his head making a butterfly crown in the air and then they flew onto the wall to make the words PJ Vlasaova. Pluto. Another bow, a flourish of his hand and he was gone.

"Way to go Pluto," said Hannah. "Now *he* was cool."

Back on the screen, the location changed to a seascape. A beach with the waves from the ocean crashing in, leaving lace patterns on the shore as they went out again. A hippie-looking lady danced (like my mum when she's had a drink at Christmas) into view.

Looking at her, I began to wonder if Megan was right and there were such beings as magical creatures. She looked like a water nymph and was dressed in pale blues and greens and had silver white hair right down her back. As she danced, she wrote on the sand with a big stick. When she'd finished, she danced off along the beach, arms swaying and on the sand we could read the words: Selene Luna. Moon child.

Megan's eyes were shining. "If she's not magic I don't know who is!"

"Yeah," said Hannah. "I *so* have to get one of these phones."

"It's not the phone. They're fairies," Megan enthused. "I'm sure they are. I *knew* they existed. I *knew* it."

"They're not fairies," I said. "They're *planets*."

Hannah and Megan looked at me with surprise.

"I thought you didn't believe what Nessa had said," said Megan. "You said you thought they were a bunch of nutters. Well they don't look like nutters to me. They look *wonderful*."

"I... I... oh..." I had surprised myself by saying so definitely that they were planets not fairies. Maybe I was being brainwashed!

"Is there anyone else on there?" said Megan and began counting on her fingers. "How many have we seen? Venus, the Sun..."

"Pluto, Saturn, the moon," Hannah continued. "That's only five. Didn't you say that there were ten?"

I nodded. I had looked them up in Will's encyclopaedia last night. "Uranus, Neptune, Jupiter, Mars and Mercury."

"Let's see, let's see," said Hannah.

At that moment, Megan glanced out of the window then got up quickly. "Oops! Come on. Our stop," she said.

"Omigod!" I exclaimed when I saw where we were. Megan was right. We'd been so immersed in the camera phone that we hadn't noticed that we'd reached the school stop already.

The bell for assembly was ringing loud and clear as we ran for the school gates. *No time to check out the other planet people*, I thought as I stuffed my phone into my rucksack. I couldn't wait to see them. Nessa had so come up trumps with her video film and my suspicion was fading again. The main feeling I had now was one of excitement.

Chapter Seven

More planets!

At break, Hannah and Georgie had to go and do library duty so Megan and I headed out into the playground. It was a lovely sunny day so we made our way over to the nearest empty bench and rolled up our sleeves ready to soak up the sun.

"I wonder which birth sign the sun is guardian for?" Megan mused as she got an apple out of her bag and started munching it.

"I'll find out," I said and got out my phone and quickly texted a message to Nessa asking which planet looked after which birth sign.

"Do you think maybe that they all hang out in Osbury?" asked Megan as we waited for Nessa to reply.

"Why would they?" I asked.

"Maybe it's like Stonehenge or Glastonbury or one of those places, you know, a sort of sacred site. That would make sense, like some places just have a good vibe and Osbury definitely does. I always like going there and you said that Nessa told you that the guy with the computer shop is one of the planet people."

"Uri. Yeah maybe," I said. "Nessa said that they are ten planets walking round in human form so I guess they have to hang out somewhere, but... how weird does this all sound?"

Megan shrugged again. "I guess it does sound odd but who really knows who anyone is or where we've come from or what it's really all about? Maybe being a Zodiac Girl is magic."

"For you maybe, but you know I don't believe in magic the way you do, Meg."

"Yes you do," she said. "You just have to open your mind to it. Magic doesn't have to be weird. It's all around us. Everywhere. We live with it every day."

"Yeah right," I said. "Megan's off in la-la land again."

"No, really, Tori," she said then she picked a pip from her apple core. "Like this, this is magic."

I patted her on the head. "Megan, my lovely, mad mate. Are you on drugs? I hate to upset you but that there is the pip from an apple."

"Ah yes. Tiny isn't it? Looks like nothing, but plant it in the ground and it will grow and grow, big, bigger than us. It will turn into a tree. A tree that bears fruit and has leaves and flowers." She held the pip up in the air. "And can you see any of that now? No. It's a pip.

An insignificant pip but from it, all that can come. No *that's* pretty magical isn't it?"

I hadn't thought about it like that before but the way she'd put it, I thought, *Wow! Actually that is magical and I've never questioned trees or flowers growing from nothing as being weird.*

"I guess. But that's nature. That's different. These tiny people in the phone and Nessa, what's that all really about, oh small-but-wise-one? I've been trying to make sense of it all morning. Like, is it some kind of astrology club and they're all members? See Megan, I was worried that Nessa might be an escaped lunatic. In fact this morning, I had decided that I didn't want anything to do with them but then… oh. I don't know what to think."

"Don't reject them," said Megan. "I think there's something special about them. There's much more to them than those people who dress up like their favourite characters from a film or a book or history. More than that. I think that you should trust them and believe Nessa when she says that they're here to help. Give me your phone again and I'll see if there are any more of them on there."

I gave her the phone and she pressed whatever she had done earlier on the bus while I looked over her shoulder.

The picture of a deli window filled the screen.

"There's one!" said Megan.

A miniature man with a very large tummy appeared from inside the shop and waved as if he could see us. He had a navy and white striped apron on and he was grinning. He pointed at a display of fabulous-looking cakes in the window and the screen zoomed in on them for a close up. One of them was covered in white icing and had words written in bright blue on it: Joe for Jupiter, it read.

"Neat," said Megan. "And those cakes look yummy scrummy."

Suddenly the screen was replaced by shiny blue curtains which opened to reveal Uri. He was on a stage and wearing the same electric blue jump suit I'd seen him in, but this time he was pedalling a unicycle around in circles and holding a bright blue umbrella in the air. With a flourish of his hand, the air filled with snow. Heavy snow coming down leaving a blanket on the ground. With one hand, he pointed at the snow and the words: Uri for Uranus appeared as if someone had written them with a stick.

"He's the guy who runs the computer shop," I said. "Uri."

"Magic," Megan breathed happily. "I sooo wish I was a Zodiac Girl. I wonder who my guardian would be. Let's see if Nessa has replied to your text."

At that moment, the phone beeped that there was

a message.

"You're Pisces right?" I asked.

Megan nodded and looked at the text. "Nessa's replied to your question," she said then read the message. "'Aries is ruled by Mars. Taurus by Venus, Gemini by Mercury, Cancer by the moon, Leo the sun, Virgo Mercury, er… Libra Venus, Scorpio Pluto, Sagittarius Jupiter, Capricorn Saturn, Aquarius Uranus and Pisces Neptune.' So that's me, Neptune would be mine."

"Let's call Nessa. And ask where he is."

Megan quickly dialled the number for Nessa then handed me the phone.

"Hey, Tori," said Nessa's voice. "Nice to 'ear from you."

"Er… hello. I'm here with my mate Megan and she's a Pisces and she wanted to know where and who Neptune is."

"No prob, lovey. He runs the fish and chip shop in Osbury," she said so I quickly relayed this information on to Megan.

"No way!" she exclaimed. "Ask about Aries. And Mars. Hannah's Aries."

"And what about Mars?" I asked Nessa.

"Mario Ares. 'E's a soldier. 'E teaches self-defence and martial arts in a church hall in Osbury. And before you ask, I run the beauty salon, also in

Osbury."

"You mean Pentangles?" I asked.

"Yeah. That's the one."

"It was on the leaflet that you gave me."

"I 'ad to make sure we met one way or another."

"And will I meet all the planets? Are they all on my phone?"

"Not all of them," she replied. "Zodiac Girls meet some of them during their time. The ones that are predominant in your chart. Okay, Got to go. Laters. Call me if you need."

"Thanks. Laters."

I clicked the phone shut and looked at Megan. "You were right. Osbury. There are loads of them in Osbury."

Megan gave me a smug look. "I know what I'm talking about more than people realize," she said.

I nodded. Maybe she did. Maybe I had dismissed her fairy stories and her theories about magic too easily.

By the time the bell went, I felt like someone had put a spoon in my brain and given it a good stir! I felt like a whole new world of people and possibilities had been opened up to me and it was really making me rethink my take on things. Maybe nothing was as it seemed and nobody who they appeared to be. I was Tori Taylor but I was also Zodiac Girl. Nessa ran a beauty salon but she was also a planet. Hah! Whatever it all meant, magic or madness, I had a feeling that my life was about to get a whole lot better.

Chapter Eight

Help!

"Oh NOOOO!" I heard Mum cry from the kitchen.

It was Monday evening and I was upstairs working on a secret birthday card for Dan whose birthday was coming up as like me, he is a Taurus. Art is the one thing that I am really good at and I often make my own cards for friends and family on special occasions. On hearing Mum, I raced down the stairs.

"What? What is it?" I asked as a feeling of panic flooded through me. Mum was sitting at the kitchen table with a letter in her hand and a pile of post in front of her. She looked pale and shocked.

She held up the letter. "I don't believe it," she said.

"What? Mum! Is it Dad? Or Gran? What's happened?"

Seconds later, Will, Dan, Andrea, Marmite and Meatloaf piled into the kitchen too. In such a small house, nothing goes unnoticed.

"My job," Mum groaned. "I've lost my job."

"But why?" asked Andrea. "Mr Lowe loves you."

"He's relocating to Scotland," groaned Mum. "We knew it was on the cards but not so soon. He never said a word about it when I was in work today."

"Coward," said Will. "He should have told you to your face."

"Mr Lowe's not very good with people," said Mum. "Only with animals. That's why he's such a good vet."

"But won't he sell the clinic?" I asked. "Someone else'll take it over surely?"

"Yeah, someone's got to look after all the local animals," said Will.

"Meow," mewed Meatloaf as if he was agreeing with Will. Sometimes I swear that cat understands what we say.

Mum nodded. "The letter says he has sold the clinic and the new vet is coming with his own full staff from his last place. My services are no longer required. No wonder he couldn't tell me to my face. He does say he's sorry though."

Dan went over to Mum and put his arm around her. "You can get another job," he said.

"Yes. Another job. Um. Let me make you some tea," said Andrea and everyone started fussing about as if tea and toast were going to make everything all right.

Ten minutes later, we were sat round munching toast and jam and wondering what to say.

"This may mean that we have to move," said Mum wearily. "I am sorry kids but… the rent went up last month and now with no job…"

"But you'll get another job," said Dan again.

"I'll try to, love," said Mum, "but there aren't many around at the moment. Mrs Nesbitt next-door-but-one was only saying last week, she and her sister had been down the jobcentre and there was nothing going. Only more cleaning work for the big agencies and they take most of the proceeds and pay their workers peanuts."

The atmosphere around the table felt as heavy as lumpy porridge. This house was tiny for the five of us as it was.

"We'll think of something, Mum," I said. "Something will turn up. When's the rent due?"

"Week on Saturday. I can just about manage that but after…"

"Then we need to put our heads together and come up with a plan," said Andrea.

Cue for Will, Dan, Andrea and I to put our heads together. Literally. It was a family joke dating back from when we were little. Will started it and it did make Mum smile to see us all leaning over with the tops of our heads touching like we were in a rugby scrum. It didn't help much though, and if any of us had nits we'd just passed them on! Ah, the joys of family sharing.

Suddenly I remembered Nessa and her gang of planet people. Who or what they were, I still wasn't sure but she did say that they were there to help.

"I may be able to do something," I said when we all sat down again.

"Oh yes. How's that?" asked Mum.

"Er… I… er, did I tell you about…? No. Um. Probably not. Where to start? Yes. The other day… No. Shut up, Tori…"

Everyone was staring at me as if I was mad. I had been about to tell them that I was a Zodiac Girl and had the aid of a bunch of aliens at my beck and call but then realized how totally crazy that would sound.

"Er… just got to go and make a phone call," I said and made a dash for the hall and up the stairs to my room where I quickly called Nessa on the magi-mobile.

"Hey Nessa," I said when she picked up. "I need your help."

"Okay. So what can I do for you?"

"My mum. She's lost her job. Can you get her another one?"

"Get your mum a job?"

"Yeah. You have a salon and Joe has a café and I've met Uri already and he has his cyber shop. Don't any of you need shop assistants or something? Mum does cleaning too."

"Oh Tori darlin', it doesn't work like that."

"But I need help and you said you could help me."

"I will. I will 'elp you but with the aspects of your chart and 'ow to deal with it. I'm 'ere to 'elp you reach your full potential."

"I'm fine. It's not me who needs help. It's Mum."

"But she's not a Zodiac Girl, Tori," said Nessa. "You are."

"But she is a Zodiac Girl's mum. And whatever affects her affects me, right? We need practical help. Not help with our aspects or potential or whatever. We might lose our home."

"'Old on," said Nessa. "I'm just looking at your chart. Hmm. A couple of encounters with Uri…"

"What does that mean?"

"Hard to predict with Uranus. It's the planet of the unexpected. It means that suprises can come like a bolt out of the blue, not that you're going to run into Uri, just 'is influence. And let's see, what else? Yeah… I did tell you that you 'ad some lessons coming up, didn't I?"

I vaguely remembered her saying something like that at the ball. "Yeah."

"So… let me see… yeah, Tori, it says you have a tough time coming up. Sorry doll, but most Zodiac Girls do. That's partly why they get chosen. I mean what's the point of 'elping someone whose life is going brilliantly? So you… looking at what's in front of me, the lesson this month is to somehow pool your resources. You have to learn not to expect miracles to fall from the sky. You have to make it 'appen."

"Make what happen?"

"Miracles. The solution to your problems. Make it 'appen."

Make it happen? I thought. *What sort of advice was that? She couldn't be vaguer if she tried.*

"You're a Taurus," said Nessa. "Did you know that all the different signs are either earth, water, air or fire?"

"No," I said. I had a feeling she was going to tell me though.

"Well they are. All the twelve signs are either fire, air, earth or water. The fire signs are Sagittarius, Leo and Aries. The air signs are Aquarius, Libra and Gemini. The water signs are Pisces, Cancer, Scorpio and the earth signs are Capricorn, Virgo and Taurus."

"So I'm an earth sign. Um… that's very nice of you to tell me Nessa but what exactly has that got to do with anything?"

"You 'ave to learn to play to your strengths, Tori. See, the earth signs are so good at being practical. Being earth signs, that means that in many respects they are just that – earthed, grounded. They 'aven't got their 'eads in the clouds like some signs. So what I'm saying sweet'eart is that being Taurus, you will be really good at doing practical things. I'm sure you'll come up with something practical as a solution."

"But like whaaaaaat?" I asked.

"Oh and 'old on a minute. Uri has message for you." She was quiet for a moment and I could hear a voice in the background. "'E says inspiration will 'it you in an unexpected way. Don't worry."

"So you can't give Mum a job then?" I asked.

"That's not what I see 'ere," said Nessa.

Useless, I thought. *Totally useless*. "Okay. Thanks," I said although I was thinking, *thanks for nothing*.

I clicked off the phone and got up to go downstairs to join the others. I felt disappointed that Nessa hadn't been more helpful so I gave the hall cupboard a swift kick with frustration as I went past. The door flew open and one of Dan's old Action Man toys fell out in front of me. I promptly tripped over it, went flying onto the carpet and landed on my stomach. I knelt up to shove the toy back in the cupboard but when I opened the door properly, a hundred things came spilling out on top of me.

"Arrrgghhhhh!" I cried as old clothes, towels, toys, magazines and games became dislodged from where they had been wedged in. Books came bouncing down from the top shelf, a box of old shoes even one of my old Barbie dolls came flying down and landed on my head. "Waaaaoooooo!"

Mum came running up the stairs. "What's going on? Are you okay, Tori?" she asked when she saw me spread-eagled on the carpet, pinned down by a baseball bat, a Monopoly board on my chest and a "Highland Fling" Scottish Barbie sitting on my head.

"Just about," I said as I rubbed my forehead.

Mum glanced up at the now half empty cupboard and the contents spilled out all over the carpet. "I guess we have been meaning to empty that out for months now," she said with a grin, "nice of you to remind us."

"Mum, I could have *died* just then."

"Yeah, right," said Mum but she didn't look very concerned. She was busy looking at the rubbish that had fallen out. "We really ought to get rid of all this stuff you know."

I could see I wasn't going to get any sympathy now that she'd seen that I was all right. All the same I decided to lie there a second more and groan. And as I lay there, it hit me. A flash of inspiration, like a bolt of lightning.

I sat up and removed Barbie's right leg from my left ear. Uri had been right. And so had Nessa. Use your resources, she had said. Inspiration will hit you unexpectedly, he had said. It couldn't be more obvious.

"I've got it, Mum," I said. "I know *exactly* what we can do to raise some extra cash."

Chapter Nine

Making the £££

I waited until I got downstairs to make my genius announcement. The others were going to be so impressed with my idea. Even I was impressed!

"Tori has an idea," said Mum to Andrea, Will and Dan who were still in the kitchen stuffing their faces with toast. "Go ahead Tori."

Mum, Andrea, Will, Dan, Marmite and Meatloaf looked at me expectantly.

"Car boot sale," I said.

Their faces dropped and Will and Dan started chomping again. Marmite and Meatloaf looked enthusiastic though, in fact Marmite hopped onto the chair nearest to me and rubbed my hand with his nose as if to show me his approval.

"Cat boot sale? Pff," said Will through a mouthful of peanut buttered toast. "No. What we need is a miracle. We need to win the lottery."

"What star sign are you?" I asked.

"Libra. Why?"

"Might have known," I said. "That's an air sign you know. Air sign for airhead. Head in the clouds. The chances of winning the lottery are like, one in a hundred billion million. We can't rely on that. We have to make our miracle happen and this is something we can practically do."

"Oo er, get her," said Dan.

"And how much do you think you're going to make from a car boot sale, dozo?" Will asked. "Fifty quid tops and how long would that last for?"

"Yeah and who would want to buy our old stuff? I bet we couldn't even give it away," said Andrea.

"Fifty quid would be better than nothing," I said. "Let's see you come up with something."

"Actually," said Mum who had been looking thoughtfully out the window after I'd made my announcement, "it's not a bad idea at all. We have got all that stuff upstairs clogging up the cupboards. And even more in the loft and in the garage. It wouldn't do any harm to get rid of it. Especially if we are going to have to move. It would give us some more space at least. And there's a car boot sale in the car park every Saturday over in Osbury. I've been meaning to check it out for bargains for some time now but I never thought of going there to sell. Yes, Tori, I think you may be on to something."

"And you could bake some of your cakes, Mum,"

I said. "People are bound to want a snack while they wander around."

Mum was beginning to look a lot more cheerful. "Yes," she said. "Let's go for it. Dan, get a piece of paper and let's make a list."

Sorted, I thought. *And it's one to you, Nessa.*

Plans for the car boot sale went into top gear. Everybody pulled together. Andrea cleared loads of her books out, Will took out a pile of old CDs, DVDs and computer games, Dan donated games and toys he'd outgrown while Mum and I found piles of old clothes and shoes we no longer wore.

I texted Nessa once the plan got under way and every day brought email messages of encouragement from her. They were so lovely, like works of art. Each one came on a pale blue background, the first had a wreath of white roses around the message, the second bright yellow sunflowers, the third a circle of ivy interwoven with white snow drops, the fourth was framed with a square made up of stars and planets that twinkled on the screen and the fifth and sixth had rows of tiny bluebirds that chirped around them. *She must be a whiz at technology and knowing how to create these pages,* I thought as I printed them out and stuck them onto my wall.

Each message was simple:

Don't give up.

Quitters never win and winners never quit.

Don't wait for your ship to come in, swim out to it.

Fortune favours the brave.

The longest journey starts with the first step.

Life is what you make it.

As the week went on, I felt as if the messages were on a loop in my head, playing over and over. Don't give up. Don't give up. Don't give up. Quitters never win and winners never quit. Quitters never win and winners never quit. Quitters never win and winners never quit... I found myself getting fired up with enthusiasm and ideas.

I so wished that I could let the other Crazy Maisies in on my plans but that would mean admitting how bad our situation was at home and I wasn't ready for that or their pity. They were off for another movie night on Saturday evening but once again I'd had to make an excuse as I didn't have the dosh. I'd said that Mum was taking me and the bros to a new restaurant in town. They didn't need to know that it may well be true, we may go to the restaurant – then help her clean it! And when Georgie asked if I was free earlier in the day to go shopping with her and her mum, I said that I couldn't because we were joining family at my uncle's country estate for a lunch party. And it was true. They were coming to help out at the car boot sale. So the country estate was really a council estate and we were meeting at a car park round the back of Mudgen's supermarket where lunch would probably be bacon sarnies, but no-one needed details.

As always when I told fibs or half lies, I felt a twinge of conscience. Sometimes I wished that I could tell them the whole story but I wasn't prepared to lose their friendship. It meant too much to me. Thankfully there were other people though who knew exactly how things were for us since Dad had left. Mum's sisters and their hubbies. And they couldn't have been more helpful.

I called Uncle Kev and he agreed to drive us to the sale in his van.

Uncle Ernie said he'd let us have some vegetables and herbs to sell on one section of the stall. His donation was on the condition that I went and helped him on his allotment some nights after school. Remembering what Nessa had said about Taureans being practical, I agreed to do it. He even said that I could have my own corner of the allotment if I wanted. I resolved to make it my new hobby for the future as I've always liked digging and planting and watching things grow. Since Megan had said that it was magic that stuff grows from nothing, I felt like my eyes had been opened to the natural wonder all around me. I'd always taken it for granted before. I think Uncle Ernie thought I was mad when I spent ages just staring at the petals of an apple blossom flower like I'd never seen one before.

Auntie Phoebe let us have a load of her old china and said anything she could do to help, she would.

Auntie Pat (who runs a beauty salon) gave us loads of skin and hair product samples.

By the end of the week, our downstairs rooms were chock-a-block ready for the sale. Even Dan, Will and Andrea were getting more enthusiastic.

Uncle Kev arrived at seven in the morning on Saturday and we all piled in his van, Mum, Uncle Kev and I in the front and the boys and Andrea wedged in with the bin bags in the back. Andrea didn't like that one bit and complained about the smell of petrol all the way there. She's such a weed, although she did look paler than her normal lily white by the time we got there.

When we got to the site, we got busy unloading the van.

"So where the table?" asked Uncle Kev when the last bag had been hauled out the back onto the tarmac.

"What table?" I asked.

"Table to lay all your stuff out on," he said.

Mum and I looked at each other with horror. All around us, professional car boot people were unfolding picnic tables and setting out their stalls. In all the activity, I hadn't thought about where we were going to put anything.

"Haven't got one," I admitted shamefacedly. "What are we going to do?"

Just at that moment, the alluring smell of frying bacon wafted towards us. Uncle Kev sniffed the air. "Yum. Bacon sarnies," he said. "Come on lads. What we need is a full stomach and then we'll deal with the problem in hand."

And off they charged without looking back! *Honestly*, I thought, *those boys do nothing else but eat, eat, eat. But bacon sarnies? What a great idea.* I could see that the lady doing the sandwiches at the back of the car park was doing a roaring trade. We had Mum's cakes but they wouldn't last long. *I should have thought of making butties. Next time, I'll be better prepared and made a mental note for my car boot sale list of essentials: Table. Sandwiches.*

"And I'm off for a cup of tea," said Mum. "Want one?"

I nodded and off *she* went leaving me alone with a pile of black bin bags and nowhere to put their contents. *I'll have to lay them out on the floor as best I can. Oh God*, I thought. *This is fast turning into a disaster.* I looked up at the sky. Clouds were beginning to gather.

"Oh *nooo*," I said to no-one in particular. "*Please* don't let it rain. No-one's going to come if it rains and Mum's cakes will go all soggy." I turned my face up to the sky again. "Zodiac Girl calling base. Zodiac Girl calling base. Help needed." I looked back at the bin bags. *Yeah right*, I thought, *like someone's going to turn up out of the blue and make it all okay. Be practical, Tori, that's what Nessa said. There isn't anyone to sort out this mess but you!*

At that moment, I saw a dark purple van drive into the site. It pulled up alongside Uncle Kev's van. Three people got out. One of them looked familiar. He was tall, very pale-looking, with a hook nose and had long hair pulled back in a ponytail. The girl with him was wearing heavy black glasses and had blonde hair scraped back in a bun and the third one was a stocky man with a shaved head. Not someone to mess with by the looks of him. They were all dressed in head-to-toe black and exuded mystery and glamour like they were the crew from a film set or something. *The tall man is one of Nessa's alien friends from the phone video, the Goth man, I'm sure of it*, I thought as he came over.

"PJ's ze name, transformation's ze game," he said and gave a low bow. "Nessa sent me for ze Zodiac Girl. Zese are my two assistants, Natalka and Oleksandra." He spoke in a foreign accent that I couldn't place. It was European but I wasn't sure from which country. He snapped his fingers and the girl and man who had accompanied him opened the back of the van and pulled out a folded table and a gazebo.

"For ze putting on of your sales items things," said PJ.

"Wow, thanks," I said.

PJ nodded and the three of them seemed to go into fast motion, like a DVD on fast forward. Ten minutes later, they had not only put up a table to put our stuff on but also assembled a small tent with open sides to go over it.

"In case of ze raining," said PJ.

"Fantastic," I said.

"Ve no finish yet," he said and with another snap of his fingers, his assistants pulled a bag out of the back of their van. It was full of balloons, flowers and coloured streamers which they set about decorating the entrance to the tent with. By the time they'd finished, our stall stood out from all the others in the car park and some of the stall holders near us were staring with open mouths.

"It's a car boot sale," said a sour-faced man who had the stall opposite, "not a blooming summer fair."

PJ raised an eyebrow and looked at the man with disdain. "Marketing, my dear sir," he said. "It iz all in ze presentation."

"Thanks so much," I said. "You saved my day."

"You're velcome," said PJ. "Nessa, she like everything to be beautiful. Iz nice to 'ave her as your guardian yes? Taureans be very luckiest. Nessa knows about making things look good." And then with a last bow, he, Natalka and Oleksandra dived back into the van and drove off.

Mum, Dan, Andrea, Will and Uncle Kev could hardly believe their eyes when they got back.

"What happened?" asked Will. He checked his watch. "We've only been gone about ten minutes. How…?"

"Friends of mine dropped by to help," I grinned back at him.

"Megan, Hannah and Georgie?" he asked. "So where are they then?"

"No, not them," I said. "Other friends."

"From school?" asked Mum.

"Er… not exactly. Um, new friends."

Mum looked puzzled. "New friends? So where have they gone? I'd like to meet them. You never told me that you'd organized this."

How can I possibly explain? I wondered. Mum was very particular about meeting the people who I mixed with.

"They had to go. Um. They're um… they're…"

"How much for the jigsaw?" interrupted a lady behind us. She was holding up a box from the table and looking directly at Mum. "Are all the pieces in there?"

"Oh yes, all complete," Mum replied.

Saved for the time being, I thought as Mum turned away and got busy serving our first customer. After the jigsaw lady, there was a constant flow of people browsing and buying and trying things on. I found an old pack of oil pastels and paper and quickly made up some colourful price tags so that prospective customers could see clearly what everything cost. As Nessa had done with the messages she'd sent in the week, I made sure that I made each one of them pretty with either a flower or a leaf or a butterfly or something to make it stand out. A few people commented on them and how attractive they were.

None of us stopped until past midday by which time we'd sold over two thirds of our stuff and Mum had forgotten all about asking after my 'new' friends. All Mum's cakes went in the first hour plus all of Uncle Ernie's vegetables and the sale couldn't have gone better apart from one dodgy moment when I spotted Sonia Marks' younger brother looking through the old CDs. I ducked down under the table before he saw me. I couldn't bear to think of him reporting back to Sonia and Chloe that I'd been seen manning a stall at a car boot sale. It would have given them the perfect excuse to sing Nickynonames again, in fact, I'd never have heard the end of it. Luckily by the time I emerged from under the table, he'd moved on.

I counted up the takings so far.

"Two hundred and fifty quid already!" I said when I'd finished.

Mum's face broke into a broad grin. "And still a pile of stuff to sell."

"So that will help with this month's rent, won't it Mum?" I said.

"More than," she smiled back. "And as it's Dan's birthday next Saturday, I'm going to throw a little party for him with some of the takings *and* I'm going to give each of you ten pounds each from the takings."

Ten quid for me! I thought. *Ace. That means I'll be able to go to the movies with the Crazy Maisies tonight without having to worry about not being able to pay my way.*

At around one, Mum suggested that Andrea and I take a break so we set off for a wander around the other stalls. Andrea wanted to look at the books and was soon getting out her share of our takings to spend. *Mad*, I thought as I left her sifting through boxes of books on one table, *she gets rid of one pile of stuff and then buys another*. I left her to it and wandered off on my own. All sorts of junk was on sale and I had a good nose round to see who was charging how much for what. I also noticed that there were stalls selling new stuff. Homemade cards, photos, frames made out of flowers, leaves and twigs, flower arrangements, home-made bath products as well as a whole variety of cakes and snacks. As I was looking at one stall with lavender pouches on it and thinking, *I could make half of the stuff I've seen*, someone tapped my shoulder. I turned to see an old man with a beard standing behind me.

I recognised him immediately. It was Dr Cronus. Saturn according to the camera phone video. He was the one who had written his name on the blackboard. He was dressed in an old-fashioned type of tweed suit and had a bright red tie with a planet and star pattern. *Neat*, I thought as I looked at his tie. *I wonder if all of the planet people wear something like that, like a secret club thing that only Zodiac members know.* Nessa had been wearing star earrings at the ball and I had noticed that Mr O had a star and planets design on his cufflinks.

"Hi," I said with a grin. "Dr Cronus I believe. I'm Tori."

He didn't return my smile. In fact he looked like he was having a major grump. "I know who you are," he said.

"So how's it going?" I asked. I couldn't help but feel a rush of excitement. If he was another of the planet people, maybe he had another surprise for me, like PJ coming and helping with the stall.

"How's it going? How's it going? What kind of grammar is that? Speak properly, girl," said Dr Cronus.

"I… I meant, you know, how are you? How's it hanging sort of thing," I replied. As the words "how's it hanging" came out of my mouth, I knew I'd said totally the wrong thing but there was something about the doctor that made me feel nervous.

Dr Cronus rolled his eyes.

No need to be so grouchy, I thought.

"So come on then, girl," he said. "I haven't come here to waste my time. What have you learnt so far this afternoon?"

"Learnt?" I said. "Nothing. It's a car boot sale," (*in case you haven't noticed*, I thought.) "We've sold loads of our stuff already."

"Yes, I went past your stall. You did the price tags, I presume?"

"I did," I said.

"Not a bad effort."

"Thanks."

"And you've had a good look around?"

I nodded.

"Notice anything?"

"Yeah. It seems to be more of a craft fair than people just selling old tat."

"Exactly," said Dr Cronus. "People using their

resources. It's inspiring, isn't it?"

I shrugged. "I guess. There's loads of stuff here that people can buy for Christmas and birthdays. Good gifts."

"*Exactly*," said Dr Cronus again. "And doesn't that make you think?"

"Think what?"

"Think Tori! About what *you* could do?"

"Me? But I've done a lot. I got our whole stall organized."

"But it needn't end here," said Dr Cronus.

I laughed. "Oh I think it will, sir, I mean doctor. We've cleared out all our cupboards and I don't think our relatives could donate any more without ending up with empty houses."

"Look around you, Tori. Look around."

I looked around. I saw the same stalls I'd looked at for the last half-hour. *Was I missing something?* I asked myself. Dr Cronus was looking at me as if he expected me to say something. "Yes. Um. Lovely. Glad the rain held off but it looks like it might shower later." What did he want to hear? Sure as beetroots were red, I didn't know and his stern stare was making me more nervous than ever.

"So have your friends from school come to help?" asked Dr Cronus.

"Who? Oh them? No. Um. Busy." His question

caught me off guard. No way was I going to admit to him that I hadn't told my mates that I was spending my Saturday selling off old stuff because basically we couldn't afford our rent and barely could afford food.

"I'd have thought they'd be here with you," said the doctor. "Be fun." He spat the word fun like it was a dirty word. *Boy, this guy is heavy going*, I thought. *He's so unlike Nessa, Uri and Mr O.*

"Nah," I shrugged. "My mate Georgie's gone shopping in town with her mum. Megan was going out to lunch with her parents to a new restaurant down on the river and Hannah's at her pony club."

Dr Cronus looked thoughtful for a moment. "New restaurant? Pony club huh?" he said. "Your friends sound well off."

I shrugged. "Kind of. Yeah, they are. Anyway, that's how they usually spend their Saturdays." I was about to add, *Which is why they wouldn't see schlepping out here as 'fun'*, but I stopped myself just in time. I didn't want this old geezer probing too much and finding out that I pretended that my Saturdays were as glam as theirs. He looked the sort that would give me a long lecture about telling the truth.

"Let them in," he said as if he had read my mind.

I pretended that I didn't know what he was talking about. "Let who in?"

"Your friends. They will understand more than you

realize. And no-one's life is ever how it seems on the outside."

"Tell me about it!" I sighed.

"Tell *them* about it."

The doctor regarded me for a few moments and I felt like he could see right into my mind and knew all that went on there. It felt really spooky and I felt myself blushing. Then all of a sudden, he looked away and almost smiled. "So what next Zodiac Girl?"

"Next? Dunno."

The half-smile faded fast. "Dunno? You mean *don't know*. I *do* wish you'd pronounce things properly. Either way, that's not going to change things is it?" he asked then sighed wearily. "I'll tell you something else about Taureans, Victoria Taylor. As well as being a sign that is good at being practical, being born under the sign of the bull can also produce the laziest of people. They *love* to sit and do nothing. See nothing. Come on Tori, *think*. What have all these stalls told you?"

"I don't know, I really don't. Can't you just tell me?" I asked.

Dr Cronus sighed again as if the whole encounter with me was exhausting him. "See? That's you being lazy and not using your brain. Okay. I *suppose* I have to spell it out to you. What's your best subject at school?"

"Art."

Dr Cronus gestured the car boot sale with a sweep of his right arm. "And do you possibly think that some of the people here might have been any good at art at school too?"

"Some of them," I said. "And others even I could do better than."

Dr Cronus nodded. "Yes, even you could. You could make most of the things here. The cards. The little paintings. The Christmas gifts. It's all in your chart. You're a very creative girl."

I gazed over at a stall over to our right. It was selling handmade cards at an extortionate price. And people were paying it, just for a bit of paper with some glitter and seeds sprinkled on it. I could do better. *Is that what he's saying?* I asked myself. *That I should be making these things? I mean, doing a car boot sale is one thing. A one-off. But was he saying that I should be making all sorts of things to sell here? Me?*

"But I'm only thirteen," I said.

Dr Cronus looked at me as if I had said something funny. "Onwee firteen," he mimicked in a little girlie voice.

"Yes. So it's not *my* responsibility to sort everything out. I'm not the grown-up."

"Not the gwown-up," he mimicked again.

For a moment I saw red. I didn't like this Dr

Cronus. I only liked the nice *friendly* planet people. I wanted to sock him.

He raised an eyebrow. "You want to hit me, don't you?"

"No," I lied.

"Yes you do," he said. "Taureans may be gentle souls most of the time but they are the sign of the bull and we all know that when a bull loses their temper, they can see red and it's best to get out of the way."

I made myself take a deep breath. "I am *not* going to lose my temper," I said but I was close to it. I'd thought that he'd understood my predicament and had come to help but he was poking fun at me and trying to make me work! Well, I wasn't going to listen. I didn't have to. Just because I was a Zodiac Girl didn't mean I had to do what old-timers like him said. *You're not my boss*, I thought.

"I'm going back to the stall now," I said and turned away from him.

He burst out laughing as I walked away.

"Oh Victoria," he called.

I glanced over my shoulder. "Yes?"

"The other thing about Taureans…"

"Yes?" I asked, but made my face looked as uninterested as I could.

"Stubborn," he said and rolled his eyes up to the sky. "Oh but they can be stubborn."

Chapter Ten

Inspiration

"Hey, how's it going with the planet people?" asked Hannah when we met up at the cinema.

"Yeah, how's it going being Zodiac Girl?" asked Megan.

I rolled my eyes. "Not as much fun as I thought," I said as we stood in line to get tickets. "I met that Saturn chap. Dr Cronus. He's picked up on the fact that I'm good at art. He was ranting on about being practical. I think he wants me to make stuff for craft fairs or something mad like that. Crazy huh?"

"How does he know you're good at art?" asked Megan.

"Oh… from my chart," I said quickly as I didn't want to say anything about the sale earlier that afternoon. "When I got home this afternoon…"

"From your lunch on your Uncle's estate?" asked Megan.

"Er… yes um that. Anyway, there were a ton of messages about websites to check out. And links to websites. I had a brief look. They were mostly for arty sites selling cards and paintings or sites with details of craft fairs in the area. I think he wants me to make nick-nack gift type things as a hobby or something. Doesn't he know that I'm a schoolgirl? That I have homework to do! Television to watch? Magazines to read? Nails to paint?"

Georgie laughed. "Yes, it's a hard life isn't it? Some people don't appreciate just how tough it is for us."

"Maybe he was trying to give you some guidance as to what you should do when you grow up," said Hannah.

"Maybe," I agreed. She might be right. Already our teachers had begun to talk about it and careers advisers had been in to give us lectures on what subjects to choose for GSCEs when the time comes. "All I know is that I want to be very, very rich."

Megan and Hannah laughed but Georgie looked sad. "Being rich isn't everything," she said. "I don't think money makes you happy. I want more than that."

"Like what?" I asked. I couldn't imagine how anybody could be unhappy if they were loaded like her.

Georgie shrugged. "Dunno. Like friends. Like people around…"

She stopped what she was saying and bit her lip.

She's upset about something, I thought and I was about to ask her more about it when Megan interrupted and I decided that maybe this wasn't the best time to ask Georgie what was going on as she looked like she was about to cry.

"Did Doctor Cronus say anything else?" asked Megan.

I shook my head. "Not really." The words "stubborn" and "lazy" rang in my head but I blocked them out for the hundredth time since he had said them. His words had struck a nerve and part of me feared that he was right. It wasn't the first time I'd been called those things, but I didn't like to think that I was like that. "Um… do you think that I'm er… lazy?" I asked.

"No more than the rest of us. Why?" asked Megan.

"Just wondered. What about stubborn?"

"Definitely," said Hannah.

Georgie and Megan both nodded in agreement with her. "Yeah," they chorused. "Very stubborn."

"What do you mean? I'm not, am I? Give me an example."

Georgie laughed. "Er… how about not coming on the school trip with the rest of us?"

I crossed my arms in front of my stomach. "Oh, that."

"Yes, that," said Megan.

"Ask your planet lady if she thinks you should go," said Hannah. "Bet she agrees with us."

She'd probably tell me to be practical or get misery guts Cronus to tell me to walk there or something equally unhelpful, I thought, but soon realized that was me being stubborn. And I didn't want to be that. *I'll ask the planet people for advice,* I thought. *I'd show them who was stubborn or not.* I had nothing to lose and I did really want to go to Italy with the others. "Hold on a sec."

"Where are you going?" asked Megan as I headed off towards the Ladies.

"Cloakroom," I called back. I wanted some privacy to text Nessa on my Zodiac phone and didn't want them looking over my shoulder.

Once in the safety of the cubicle, I got the phone out of my rucksack and typed in my question. "Need £££ for ski trp to pasta land. Ny sgestns?"

A message came back seconds later. "Use ur talents."

I texted back. "M a schlgrl. Dnt hv tme."

A message came back. "Excuses."

I had a feeling that Dr Cronus was somehow hogging the line. I texted back. "Isnt thre ny1 else thre bsdes Saturn?"

This time, there was no return text but a minute later, my phone rang. It was Nessa. *Phew,* I thought.

"Okay," she said. "I checked over your chart again.

There was the encounter with Pluto and Saturn earlier today. 'ow did you get on?"

"PJ's way cool," I said, "but Dr Cronus isn't exactly a bundle of fun is he?"

Nessa laughed. "Oh, 'e 'as 'is moments but I did tell you that 'e's known as the task master of the zodiac. The one who 'as lessons to teach. Listen to what 'e 'as to say, Tori. It's for your own good and 'e's on the level, really 'e is."

I wonder if he ever gets on to her about dropping her H's when she speaks, I wondered but decided not to ask. "I get enough lessons at school. Isn't there anything else in my chart? Anything nice?"

"Everybody's chart is a mixture," Nessa replied. "But it's what you make of it that makes the difference and makes it nice or not. Sometimes what you resist, persists. But 'old on, there is a good aspect to Jupiter comin' up, that should be okay."

"That's Joe isn't it? Jupiter. The one with the deli. Jupiter's the planet of jollity and expansion isn't it?"

"On the nail, darlin'," said Nessa.

"So what does that mean then? A good aspect to Jupiter?"

"Well, where it's placed in your chart usually means good luck of some sort. It can mean winnings out of the blue or unexpected windfalls."

I punched the air. That was more the sort of thing

I wanted to hear. Better than old Cronus's ideas. "Excellent."

"And I was thinkin' about your Italy trip," said Nessa. "Why not suggest to one of your teachers that they 'old a raffle? With the money raised, maybe it can sponsor one student on the trip."

Ya-ay, I thought. *What a totally brill idea. Nessa is so nice. I am so glad that she's my guardian and not old killjoy.* I had a feeling that as the idea had come from Nessa and *I* was her Zodiac Girl and Jupiter was jolly and about windfalls and such, that I would win if there was a raffle. That was what she was trying to tell me. I just knew it.

"Thanks, Nessa."

"That's what I'm 'ere for innit? And come by and meet Joe some time," she said. "He runs the deli in Osbury. Bring your mum. They can talk cakes. He always loves to meet a fella cook."

"Okay, will do." I said. *I might leave out the fact that he's supposedly the planet Jupiter here in human form though,* I thought. *Mum would think I had been taking drugs if I told her that.*

As I went out to join the others, my mouth fell open. Who was standing there outside the cinema as if she was waiting for someone? Our teacher, Miss Creighton! I could hardly believe my eyes. It was clearly meant to be. Part of a plan. Part of a "get Tori to Italy" plan. *Magic*, I thought as I went straight out to her and told her about the raffle idea.

"Excellent idea, Tori," she said. "I'll get it organized first thing on Monday morning as there are a couple of places still not taken. What a clever girl you are."

I beamed back at her. *Italy here I come*, I thought.

Chapter Eleven

Acceptance

I beamed out at the envious faces in front of me. "Thank you so much for this wonderful prize," I said and then smiled modestly. "And I can assure you I shall do my very best to have the most fantastic time ever."

And then everyone would cheer as I got down from the stage with my ticket to Venice in my hand.

That was my fantasy anyway. Soon to become a reality.

True to her promise, Miss Creighton had put the raffle plan into effect and she confided in me that there had been a fantastic response. By Thursday, she said that there was enough in the kitty to send at least one pupil on the trip. I knew the prize was mine not only because Nessa had hinted at it but also on Monday night, a message had come through from old Cronus-socks. "Learn acceptance," it said.

I knew exactly what he meant and so every evening after school, in front of the mirror on my chest of drawers in my bedroom, I practised my acceptance speech. I tried a variety of expressions for when Miss Creighton announced that the winning ticket was mine. Surprise. Quiet dignity. Just a smile. Modest but thankful.

"What on earth are you doing?" asked Will on Friday morning. I'd left my bedroom door ajar and he caught me at it. It was the day of the draw and I still hadn't decided what expression to go for when I was announced as the winner and called up in front of the school.

"Say one won something fab," I said. "How do you think one ought to look?"

"One? Who's one?"

"Me duffhead. Say I'm one. The one. Say I won something. How should I look when it's announced."

Will shrugged. "Dunno. Don't care. Why? What are you expecting to win?"

"A holiday."

"Can I come?"

"No."

"How do you know you've won or that one's won?"

"Because Jupiter is favourably aspected in my horoscope."

"Oh *that* rubbish," he scoffed. "Astrology's a load of cobblers you know. Some stupid journalist is paid to make it all up so that suckers like you will read your horoscope in the paper and think that their lives are going to improve."

"That's not true. At least not all of it. The stuff you read in the papers might be made up but if you have your own personalised birthchart done then it's actually scientific."

"Yeah right. How do you know?"

I didn't know but I wasn't going to tell him that. "I know because my brain is far superior to yours on account of the fact that I am a girl. So come on. You must have an opinion. Okay. This is me being told the prize is mine."

I quickly ran through my practised expressions for him. Surprise. Joy. Dignified acceptance etc. He burst out laughing.

"Looks like you've eaten something dodgy and need the loo really badly," he said.

I rolled my eyes up to the ceiling. "I don't know why I bothered to ask you."

"Okay, you should do it like those people on the Oscars, I guess. Just don't start blabbing like a baby and thanking everyone from your parents to the milkman."

"Tori, can you come here a moment?" Mum called from her bedroom.

I grabbed my rucksack and went to see what she

wanted. She put a finger up to her lips, beckoned me inside her room and shut the door.

"What's the big secret?" I asked.

"Dan," she said. "I've put a birthday present aside for him at the cyber café shop in Osbury. You know the one with the computers at the back and the novelty items at the front. It's a computer game that he's had his eye on for ages." She handed me a twenty pound note. "I called yesterday and said that someone would be in to collect the game tonight. I might not finish work until the shop is shut so can you pop over there after school?"

I nodded. "Sure. I know exactly where the shop is."

"Excellent," said Mum. "And we'll have a lovely time tomorrow hey? You have invited the Crazy Maisies to the party haven't you?"

"Er… I think they're busy," I said, "but I'll try again."

I hadn't asked them because, as always, I didn't want to take the risk of one of them asking too many questions about when the house would be finished and blowing my cover. What they didn't know about, they wouldn't miss.

Mum gave me the money and after a last check in the mirror, I set off for school. I couldn't wait. In just over an hour, my place on the school trip would be secure. I had already laid out the clothes that I was going to take and earlier in the week at school, I had happily joined in with all the talk about where we were going to go and what we were going to see and what we were going to wear. I'd wear my Susie Tsang dress, it would look so cool with some black shades. And I'd buy some red lipstick. I'd seen models in the glossies wearing it really bright this year. Cherry red was the new red.

The rest of the Crazy Maisies didn't know that my only chance of going was the raffle. They thought it was a done deal and that I'd changed my mind after the movie outing and signed and paid up like they had. It would be okay when they saw me win the prize. I'd just explain that I wanted to support the raffle.

Assembly was the usual boring mix of announcements and readings then at last, Miss Creighton took the microphone and the hall grew quiet. She was carrying a small hat that she put on the podium in front of her.

As she looked out at the expectant faces, I took a deep breath and tried to calm the rising feeling of excitement.

"I know a lot of you have been waiting for this morning and I'm not going to keep you in suspense much longer although I would like to thank everyone for the fantastic response we've had. So now… the name of the person with the winning ticket."

She put her hand in the hat and pulled out a ticket.

"And that person is…" The silence seemed to go on forever. And ever. And *ever*.

I had to hold myself back from heading for the stage.

"Jane Brightman," said Miss Creighton at last.

I almost fell over as one of my feet set off for the stage and the rest of my body held back. A cheer went up from the other side of the hall and a flushed Jane Brightman went up onto the stage.

I was stunned and I'm sure my face registered an expression *not* practised in the mirror that week. Horror!

"You all right?" asked Georgie. "You looked like you were about to fall over."

I nodded. "Umpf. Felt a bit faint… Didn't have any breakfast…"

My stomach sank and I felt as if my heart was about to break as my fantasy disappeared before my eyes and became a reality in front of Jane's. Now I knew what Dr Cronus's message had really meant. Prepare for acceptance. Acceptance that *someone else* had won my freaking prize. Messages from Dr C really were a bad omen.

Chapter Twelve
Planet Earth to Tori

The rest of the day at school went by in a blur as my mind went through my options – or lack of them. What was I to tell the girls now that there was no way that I could go to Italy? I'd have to fake illness or insanity. Or both. Something. Maybe it was for the best. Maybe winning the ticket wouldn't have been enough anyway. There was still other stuff I'd have needed for the trip: clothes, make-up, snack money, mags for the plane. Mum could never have given me the money for that. If I was realistic, it had all been a dream. That's what I had to accept. Never mind planets in the sky. I had to come down to where I really was. Planet earth to Tori. I was a poor girl from a poor family.

Megan, Hannah and Georgie were very sweet to me all day, like they knew that something was wrong but couldn't figure what. They fell for my "not feeling well" line and shared their sweets at breaktime and Hannah did my nails at lunch. And Georgie and

Megan tried to make me laugh by doing the zombie shuffle dance that I had invented last Christmas. It involved making your eyes cross, letting your mouth go slack like you're going to dribble, bending the knees slightly then shuffling along slowly in a line. We always ended up on the floor laughing whenever we did it and seeing Georgie and Meg trying so hard and acting so mad did make me smile, but underneath their being nice to me only made me feel worse. I didn't deserve friends like them.

Dr Cronus had clearly foreseen what was going to happen, I thought. *At least he tried to warn me. And maybe he had been trying to help with his suggestions about me making money through my art.*

I played over my conversation with him again to see if I had missed something. And what had Nessa said about Jupiter? Unexpected windfalls. What was that all about?

At lunch break, I checked my mobile to see if there were any other messages on there. Anything that would give me a clue as to what to do next.

There were three voicemails.

Two from Nessa. Her first said, "Your moon is in Cancer, Tori. This means an emotional time." *That probably refers to just now in assembly,* I thought, *that was waaaaay emotional.*

The second message said: "It's not over until it's

over."

Did that mean there was hope? It wasn't over yet? I didn't know any more.

I listened to the third message. It was from Mr O. "Take a chance," he said.

Take a chance. On what? The raffle was over. I hadn't won despite my good aspect to Jupiter. I was beginning to think that Will was right. Astrology was for suckers. And I was sucker of the week.

As the afternoon classes droned on, I played and replayed everything that had happened since I'd been told that I was a Zodiac Girl. Despite everything, I did want it to mean something. Maybe I'd missed what they were trying to tell me.

Take a chance. Take a chance? What did Mr O mean by that? And then it hit me. Of course! It wasn't the raffle I was meant to win. It never was. That was just to show me that things could happen. Unexpected things. But I had to *make* what I wanted happen.

I could hardly wait for school to be over so that I could get out and put my plan B into operation. Mission millionaire. I knew *exactly* how I was going to do it.

"Aren't you coming for a cafe latte?" Megan called after me as I charged out of school gates. "We're going to Maxwells."

"Later," I said. "Got to pick up something for Mum, for Dan. Sorry. Urgent."

I raced off towards the bus stop leaving the girls looking at me with puzzled expressions on their faces. I didn't want to say too much in case they decided to tag along and I didn't want any witnesses when I put my plan into action.

I got the bus to Osbury and once there, headed for the nearest newsagent. *When this works out, I'll go and meet this Joe Jupiter person*, I thought as I opened the door to the shop and went in.

"Yes, young lady," said the man behind the counter.

I counted my money out. I had the twenty pounds that Mum had given me for Dan's present and four pounds left from my car boot sales money. I took a deep breath. *It's now or never*, I thought. *Take a chance.*

"Yes, young lady?" said the man again.

For a moment, I almost turned on my heel and ran out of the shop but a voice in my head was urging me on. *Take a chance, take a chance, take a chance. I had to be Zodiac Girl for some reason*, I thought. *So I shouldn't chicken out now. Now is my chance to change my life. And that of my family.*

I handed the money to him. "Twenty four scratch cards please."

The man regarded me with suspicion.

"For my mum," I said.

"How old are you?"

"Sixteen," I lied. "Anyway, the cards are for my mum."

The man briefly glanced out of the window and I sensed that he was having doubts about selling them to me but suddenly he sighed. "Feeling lucky is she, your mum?"

"No. I am. Um… that's why she sent me."

"Right then. Which ones do you want? Lucky stars or tombola."

I almost burst out laughing. It was *obvious* which ones I should pick. "Oh lucky stars," I grinned back at him.

"Do you want the ones for the top prize of fifty thousand or one hundred thousand?"

"One hundred thousand."

He peeled off cards and gave them to me. "Tell your ma to lend us a fiver if she wins," he said with a wink.

"I'll do that," I said.

Once outside, I scanned the green for somewhere private where I could go and see how much I had won. I could hardly wait.

At the other end of the village was a church and a church hall and next to that was the bus shelter. *That'll do*, I thought and set off as fast as I could.

The shelter smelt damp and musty from last night's rain but I found myself a corner and set about scratching. The amounts you could win varied: £1, £10, £100, £1000 or £100,000.

I could hardly breathe with excitement as I scratched off the first card. One star appeared. I only had to get three stars and I'd get a prize. I scratched again. A cherry. And a square. Nope this card wasn't my lucky one.

Never mind. I had twenty three more to go. One of them was bound to be a winner. *Maybe even more than one*, I thought as a rush of excitement surged through me.

Onto the next.

One star. A square. And a circle.

Next.

Two lemons and a square.

On I scratched. Triangles. Squares. Circles. Cherries. Lemon but no more stars until there was only one Scratch card left.

"Please, please let this be the one," I prayed. "Please let Jupiter and his aspects work some magic."

I scratched my last card. A star. *Another* star. Omigod, this was going to be it. Two stars. I only needed one more. I scratched away the remaining square as my heart beat in my chest. A... a circle. A circle? *Nooooooooo.* It *couldn't* be. I stared hard at the card. Two stars and a circle. *Maybe I've missed the winning card. Been too much in a hurry?* I thought as I went through them again. But no. None of them had the required three stars. I hadn't even won one *single* pound.

"NOOoooooo," I yelled as I ripped up the cards and threw them in the bin. Then I kicked the side of the bus shelter. Unfortunately it was just as an old man went past. He gave me a filthy look. "Stupid young vandals," he muttered as he shuffled on.

I felt like crying. *I am not a vandal*, I said to myself. *I really really am a loser now. And oh god, I've gambled away Dan's birthday present money. How am I going to explain that away? Oh God, oh God, oh God.* I felt as if my insides had turned to stone, heavy, solid. What was I going to do? I couldn't go home. I couldn't go to my friends. I'd lied to them too. Sooner or later they were going to find out that I wasn't going to Italy. And never had been.

I watched the old man dodder along the path, still muttering. *What does he know about my life?* I thought. *What does anyone know about my life and what it's like being me and how much I try. Try to have friends when I can't really keep up with them. Try to be cheerful for Mum when really I'm worried about her and the fact we might have to move. It's very hard being me and keeping up all the pretence.*

And as for being a Zodiac Girl, what a load of old hogwash that is. I was stupid getting those scratch cards and I was stupid thinking that being a Zodiac Girl might make me special and I was stupid to believe Nessa's insane story that she and the others were actually planets here in human form.

I almost laughed out loud when I thought how stupid I had been. Far more stupid than Megan and her fairies.

I suddenly felt very tired. Exhausted. I felt like lying under the bench in the bus shelter and going to sleep right there. And never waking up. Tears sprang to my eyes and slowly dripped one by one down my cheek. I hadn't even got the energy to cry properly. *No-one knows about my life and how unhappy I am sometimes, I thought. No-one. Not Mum. Not Andrea. Not Will. Nor Dan, nor Megan, nor Georgie, nor Hannah.*

As I sat there, it was as if a damn burst and all the feelings that I'd been holding back came rushing to the surface and I began to sob. I felt so stupid. Gambling away the only bit of money I had and Mum's too. Hard earned cash from the car boot sale. I so should have known better. *I'm so lonely, I thought. I kid myself that I have friends but they don't know the real me. The poor me. The liar me. They'd hate me if they knew what I was really like. No wonder Dad didn't want to live with me any more. I'm despicable.*

When he walked out on us, for a long time I felt that it was my fault. I never told anyone because I didn't want to have it confirmed. But it's what I felt. My fault. Dads don't leave their children. Not without good reason. And not only did he leave. He went to the other side of the world. And he hardly ever phones. *He can't love me very much can he?* I thought.

As I sat there blubbing, I heard my Zodiac phone ring. I let it ring and ring. "I'm not answering you," I said to it. "Fat lot of good being a Zodiac Girl has been to me. In fact, if it wasn't for you, I wouldn't be in this stupid mess."

I chucked my phone in the bin where I'd thrown the useless scratch cards.

Planet earth to Tori, I heard a voice in my mind say. *That's where you belong, down on the ground, not up in the stars. Yes. Planet earth to loser.*

Chapter Thirteen

All Alone

Five o'clock went by.

Six o'clock.

Seven.

I sat in the bus shelter and felt as if I couldn't move. Frozen in time. Inside I felt numb. Empty. Outside I felt cold. And... *hungry*. God, I was hungry.

But I wasn't going home. I wasn't going anywhere. I was going to stay here until moss grew over me and my skin rotted away and my bones turned to sand. *Urghh, what a horrible image*, I thought as a fresh wave of tears welled up inside of me.

A few people walked by. A couple of them stared at me but then moved on. The sky turned grey and it began to drizzle.

As the light began to fade, I looked up into the sky. The rain passed leaving a clear night, with stars beginning to twinkle and over the horizon was the silver light of a crescent moon. *I wonder what's really out there*, I thought. I felt so small and insignificant sitting there. *More planets, stars, galaxies? More people like me sitting somewhere on another bench in a bus shelter up in space in a parallel universe? Sad and lonely, like me?*

I looked down from the sky and saw a lady with long, silver hair coming across the green towards me. She was dressed in a long, sea-green skirt and aquamarine top. I recognised her straight away. Selene Luna. The Moon. *Oh noooooo*, I thought. *Well you can take a hike missus, I've had my fill of your lot.* I sooo didn't want anyone to see me in the state I was. I was sure I looked a right mess with a swollen nose and bloodshot eyes. And I didn't want anyone feeling sorry for me either.

As she reached the shelter, I was ready to tell her to go away but she didn't say anything. Not a word. She gave me the briefest nod then sat down next to me. She sighed and then to my great surprise, she started blubbing. Blubbing for Britain, blubbing like she was going for the Olympic gold.

I looked around and across the green to see if there was anyone who might know her. Might have upset her. But the landscape was completely deserted. Not a soul in sight.

It stopped me crying that was for sure. No way I could compete. She was sobbing so hard a bubble of snot blew out the end of her nose. *Eeww, impressive*, I thought as I fished about in my pocket, found a tissue and handed it to her. She gave her nose a good blow, sighed a heavy sigh then turned to look at me at last.

She still didn't say anything.

"I... I... know how you feel," I said.

That set her off again. This time, she managed two snot bubbles. One out of either nostril.

I'd never seen an adult with nose bubbles before. Only toddlers and the sight of hers gave me the giggles. I tried my best to hold them in but as always when I know I'm not supposed to laugh, it always makes me want to laugh all the more. I clenched my jaw, I wriggled my shoulders, I breathed out heavily but I couldn't suppress it and out came an explosion of laughter.

She turned on me immediately. "What's so funny?"

"Nothing," I said. "Nothing. Really. I'm sorry. Just... oh it's been a mad day and here... well here we are sitting in the bus shelter, me crying, you crying..." I pointed vaguely at her nose.

She followed my pointing finger and went cross-eyed as she focused on the end of her nose. That made me want to laugh even more but I wasn't sure how she was going to react so once again, tried to hold it in. *Oh please don't start crying again*, I thought as her face looked like it was about to crumple. But she didn't. She started to laugh too. And that set me off again. Big time. We both sat there and had a really good laugh. It felt great.

When we were both laughed out and cried out, she got up.

"I'll be off then," she said.

"Right then," I said.

And that set us off *again*. Laughing our heads off like loonie petunies.

Then she bent over, pulled my phone out of the bin, handed it to me and whispered, "Never be afraid of your feelings Tori Taurus and never be afraid to let them out and share them. Now go home. Be yourself. Tell the truth. It's all going to be all right."

I nodded. Yeah right, like I was going to take advice from a nut job (which she clearly was). But maybe I would go home and confess all. I had nothing left to lose.

After she'd gone, I got out a tissue and blew my nose. I had a quick look at my phone to see who had been trying to call earlier. Missed call from Dr Cronus, it said. *No loss there then*, I thought as I stood up and glanced over at the row of shops opposite. I wasn't ready to go home and face the music just yet. I could see Pentangles, the salon that Nessa owned. Maybe I could go and see if she was there but there were no lights on when I walked over and looked in the window. At that moment, the smell of cooking wafted past my nose. Onions. Garlic. Whatever it was, it smelt delicious and reminded me that I was hungry.

The smell was coming from the deli that Nessa had spoken about. As I moved along the street, I could see that inside there were several customers tucking into steaming plates of pasta at tables covered in red and white clothes. Just watching them made my mouth water. It looked cosy and warm in there but I had no money left to go in. I'd gambled it all away.

With a rumbling tummy, I moved on. The next shop along was Uri's cyber café and as I passed by, I felt a stab of guilt. *How could I have spent the money for Dan's present, that really was the lowest of the low.* I'd have to find a way to make it up to him. Offer to do his homework for the next few years. Let him have the TV remote from now until eternity. Sit in the comfy red seat. Make him cheese and tuna toasties every night. Be his slave. *I'll do anything*, I thought, *as long as he forgives me.*

The shop was shut but in the window were a couple of state-of-the- art TV sets that caught my eye. Both were switched on and were showing what appeared to be a lecture in a hall. The lecture was being given by an elderly man with a beard. It was my old pal. Dr Cronus. *There's no getting away from him*, I thought as I began to listen to what he had to say.

"And so in life," said Dr Cronus from the TV, "one of the major lessons to be learnt is that a person must make their own luck."

"Oh here we go again," I groaned.

"Who are you talking to, dingbat?" asked a familiar voice. I span around to see Will standing there with Stu, his tall, gangly mate from school.

"The man on the telly," I said. "He said that a person must make their own luck. Listen to him droning on." I could hear Dr Cronus continuing his speech. "Get up and make it happen blah blah blah." Similar stuff to the messages that Nessa had sent me before the car boot sale.

Stu and Will were looking at me as if I was mad. Will tapped the shop front window. "D'er, glass. Probably double-glazed. How can you hear what he's saying?" he asked.

"By listening, idiot. Why? Can't you hear?"

Will and Stu both shook their heads but I could hear Dr Cronus as clear as if he was standing right next to me.

"Probably because your ears are full of stuffing," I said.

Stu strained to listen but shook his head. "Nope, still can't hear anything. You can read lips, can't you?"

"No," I said. "I can hear what he's saying. Can you really *really* not hear him?"

Will shook his head again.

"She's winding you up," said Stu and sloped off down the pavement.

"I'm not," I said.

But Will had got bored too and followed his friend. *Maybe they were winding me up*, I thought as they disappeared around a corner, *and they could hear him and are trying to make me think that I'm losing my mind. That's the sort of sad thing that boys like to do for a laugh.*

Only one way to find out, I decided as a middle-aged lady approached.

"Er excuse me but can you hear what that man on the television in that window is saying?" I asked and pointed at the display.

She looked at the window then back at me as if I was mad. "No. No, I can't," she said and hurried off like she couldn't get away from me fast enough.

I was about to follow the boys when I heard a noise coming from the window, I turned back to see Dr Cronus knocking on the television screen. "Oi, you. I haven't finished with you yet! Yes, you Victoria Taylor."

"You can... you can *see* me?" I said.

The miniature Dr Cronus in the television set nodded. "Yes, I can see you, I tried calling before but there was no answer. Now, are you taking in what I'm trying to tell you?"

"Yes. No. *What?*" I asked.

"Make it happen," he said. "Use your talents."

I looked up to the sky. It had grown cloudy again.

"Yeah, yeah, so you said."

Dr Cronus looked angry. He reached out of the television screen and switched himself off. As the visual on the TV faded, I heard him call two words. "Lazy. Stubborn."

"You DON'T UNDERSTAND," I yelled back at the shop window causing yet another passer-by to look at me as if I was bonkers.

I may as well go home, I thought and made my way across the green. As I stood waiting for the bus, I did some serious thinking. Things were going to change. I was going to change. I couldn't go on the way I had been. I was sick of the lying. And I wanted friends to like me for who I really was. Nickynonames, the discount diva. Me. Not who I pretended to be.

In the distance, I could see a bus approaching. *Just in time*, I thought as the green lit up with a flash of lightning followed moments later by a rumble of thunder.

As I got ready to flag down the bus, to my left, I saw a chubby man running towards me. He reached me just before the bus arrived and thrust two small bags into my hand.

"Two gifts to help you on your way," he said in a Greek accent. "A package for your brother from Uri. The other from me. No charge for either."

"For me? Oh! Thanks."

"You're welcome. You have made good resolutions to be brave."

"But how do you…?"

He tapped the side of his nose, stuck out his hand and waved the bus down. When it stopped, the doors opened and he ushered me on. A moment later, it began to pour down.

It was only when I was in my seat that I realized who the chubby man was. Joe. Jupiter. I looked to see what was in the bags. In one was the computer game for Dan and in the other the most delicious vanilla slice I had ever tasted in my life. My unexpected windfall had arrived after all.

Chapter Fourteen
Dan's day

I made three calls when I got home.

Luckily Mum was still at work when I walked through the front door and Andrea and Dan were so absorbed in a movie that they hardly registered that I was back or even that I was late.

I quickly went to find the phone in the kitchen and called Hannah, Megan and Georgie. I invited each of them to Dan's birthday party. "… it's a last minute thing really, Mum decided to do it as a surprise which is why I couldn't let you know earlier." I said as I vowed to myself that was the last lie I was ever going to tell. "And I… I have something really important to tell you afterwards."

"Sounds serious," teased Georgie.

"It is," I replied.

The next morning was a hive of activity in our house. Will whisked Dan out of the way to play some early morning footie practice and the rest of us got stuck in getting everything ready for the party.

Uncle Kev arrived and Mum was straight out down the shops with him to get supplies. Aunt Pat and Phoebe came soon after they'd gone and started baking and preparing food. Uncle Ernie and cousin David put up the gazebo that we'd used at the car boot sale in the garden. Andrea was in charge of decorations and I went from room to room mucking in where ever I could.

By the time it was twelve o'clock, the house looked festive and bright and all our efforts were worth it when Will brought Dan back. His face lit up to see what everyone had done for him and when he got his presents, he looked like he was going to burst. *This is the best*, I thought. *Seeing people that I love happy*. Inwardly I thanked Joe for giving me the computer game. I would have hated myself today if Dan hadn't got it because of my stupidity.

Guests arrived: more relatives and their kids, Megan, Georgie, Hannah, neighbours, more friends and the party was soon in full swing. Will and a bunch of his mates dressed up as clowns and put on a hilarious show for the younger kids and Megan, Hannah and Georgie looked as if they were enjoying it all as much as the five year-olds.

I was so pleased that they'd come as I'd thought that they may have had far more glamorous things to do but all of them had leapt at the chance when I asked them last night. As I watched them larking about, the thought of what I had to do and say made me catch my breath with fear. Today was the day that I was going to come clean with them. Tell them the whole story, the truth about me and my family. If they ditched me then so be it, I had no-one to blame but myself.

As the afternoon wore on, the food got eaten, people began to tire and the grown ups all went inside for a cup of tea and 'to put their feet up' while some of the younger ones played tag at the end of the garden. Will and his mates went into the sitting room to watch telly and Dan and his mates went up to his bedroom to try out the computer game.

That left me with Megan, Hannah and Georgie at the tables at the top of the garden. I began to clear a few things away, stack plates and put leftovers in a bin bag but I knew that the moment would come sooner or later.

And it did.

"So what was it that you wanted to talk to us about?" asked Megan.

"Oh…" I started. The three of them were all staring at me so earnestly that I almost lost my nerve. "I… I… I'm not who you think I am," I blustered.

Hannah laughed. "Who are you then?"

"No. I mean, I *am* Tori. Tori Taylor, it's just that… well… I've…" *This is soooooooo difficult,* I thought. *The most difficult thing I have ever done in my whole life.* "I've… Look, I'm just going to come right out and say it and I hope you won't hate me forever. Okay. Here goes. Right. I'm a liar. And a loser. And…"

"No," said Georgie. "Not a loser."

"And *not* a liar," said Megan.

"Yeah. What are you talking about?" asked Hannah. She looked around with a puzzled expression on her face. "Is this some kind of pretend game?"

"No. I wish it was. I *am* a liar. You don't know," I said. I held out my arms and indicated the house. "For starters, my family is poor. My Mum's poor. She does three jobs. Or at least did. She was made redundant from one of them last week. We may have to move. And… and the decorators have never been in." As the truth came tumbling out, I felt my voice wobble as tears threatened to spill out. "We… we couldn't afford decorators. And my Uncle hasn't got a country estate. He lives in a council estate a few miles away. And I haven't got any of the things that I said I had and I can't afford designer clothes. I am Nickynonames. I get my clothes from charity shops. We get *loads* of stuff from charity shops. Books, CDs, games. And I can't afford to go to Italy either. Never could. I have *nothing.* Not even a dad. He went to the other side of the world and hardly gets in touch. He even forgot Dan's birthday today…" The thought of that made my eyes fill up with the tears I'd been holding back and all the girls reached out but I crossed my arms. "Don't be nice. I don't deserve it. I am the *worst* friend in the whole world."

Megan ignored what I'd said and stepped forward and gave me a huge hug. "No, you're not."

"Why didn't you tell us all this?" asked Georgie. "We are your friends after all."

"Because I thought you'd feel sorry for me because I couldn't keep up. And think I was a loser."

Georgie rolled her eyes. "As *if.*"

"Yeah, as if," Megan and Hannah chorused.

The three of them stood there staring at me then they looked at each other then back at me. I looked back at them.

It was Georgie who spoke first. "Well, I don't care if you're poor," she said.

"Me neither," said Megan. "I don't hang out with you because of where you live or what you wear."

"Me neither," said Hannah. "I just like you."

"Really?" I gulped back the huge sob rising up in my throat. "Bu… bu… bu…" I tried to hold it back but then I remembered what Selene had said last night in the bus shelter in the rain. Share your feelings. Out came the sob and tears spilled down my cheeks.

"Hon... hon... honest?"

The three of them nodded. "Honest."

"And... but... can you forgive me?"

They nodded again. "For what?" asked Georgie.

"For not being honest with you."

"Forgiven," said Hannah.

"Group hug," said Megan and the three of them surrounded me and hugged me.

When they released me, Georgie said, "Now that this is all out, I have something to ask you."

My heart sank. *Oh no*, I thought, *She's going to ask me something embarrassing and I'm going to have to confess to even more awful things I've done and said!*

I decided to try and be brave and face all the music. "Okay, what is it?" I asked.

Georgie glanced back at the house. "Er... well... can we... that is... can I come over here more often?"

"*Here?* Yes. But why? I mean of course but... I never thought you'd want to. I mean your house is fab and..."

"Empty," said Georgie and for a moment, she looked sad. "I hate going back there after school. Neither Mum or Dad get home until past nine some days and yes, okay, the housekeeper's there but it's not the same. That's why I always love coming here. There are people about and the house looks lived in. And your brothers are fun. At our house, it's so clinical. You daren't relax in case you spill a crumb. I reckon here a person can be themselves and even act mad if they feel like it. I looooove it here. I love that your aunts and cousins come over to help out. I love that you dress up in silly costumes to watch movies. My house is…" And then *her* eyes filled up with tears, "lonely."

"Group hug," I said and we all hugged again.

When we pulled back, Megan looked at Hannah. "Anything you need to get off your chest, dear?" she said with a big smile.

Hannah looked thoughtful for a moment. "I've always been afraid that you guys might drop me because I'm not as pretty as you are."

"No way," I cried. "You are *so* pretty but more than that, you're fun."

Hannah blushed and I swear for a moment that she looked tearful too.

"Megan? You okay?" asked Georgie.

"Yeah. I guess. Except… okay, seeing as we're all being honest here," she said as she shifted about on her feet and looked awkward. "Sometimes I think I'm not as… well… interesting or funny as the rest of you…"

"Noooo waaaay," Hannah, Georgie and I cried and then we chorused, "group hug."

We had another group hug then Megan said, "Zombie shuffle."

Immediately we lined up, made our eyes cross, our mouths slack, bent our knees and began to shuffle around the garden. In seconds, we all had the giggles and Georgie lost her footing and toppled over. Megan went over her, Hannah tripped over her and they pulled me down as well. We lay on the ground in a heap and laughed like drains.

Will leant out of the window and yelled, "Any room for boys in there?"

Georgie blushed this time and gave Will a coy look as she got up and smoothed her skirt down. *Ah! I see exactly why she loves it round here*, I thought, but I didn't mind. From what the girls had said, it looked like I wasn't the only one who was worried and I wasn't the only one with hang-ups that they were afraid to tell anyone about. I made a vow to myself that in future, I'd be more aware of what my friends were going through and not just think about me and my problems. And I'd be more honest with them about everything.

Later that evening, Auntie Pat called everyone into our front room and Mum brought in the cake that she'd made for Dan. She'd made it in the shape of his favourite chair and iced it in bright, red icing.

"Your very own comfy chair," said Mum.

"Cool," he said.

After he'd blown the candles out then cut the cake,

Aunt Phoebe passed pieces around to everyone.

"Hey, you know what your mum ought to do as a job?" asked Georgie as she munched on her bit.

"What?" I asked.

"Party organiser," she said. "My mum pays a fortune for people to come and do hers and sometimes, I don't think they're that brilliant. Today has been the best ever. Great food, great entertainment. Your mum would be ace at it."

"Yeah," said Megan. "And you could design the invites and things."

"Or makes cards," said Hannah. "Birthday cards like the ones you make us."

And suddenly I understood what old Cronus-boots had been on about. I could see it all in my mind's eye. Taylor's Terrific Times: birthdays, bar mitzvahs... you name it, we could cater for it...

"Hey Mum," I said. "Georgie's got a great idea for how you, that is we, could earn some dosh..."

Epilogue

Taylor's Terrific Times was set up in June of that year after a trial run on my birthday in May. We took advantage of the date coming so soon after we'd made the decision to go into business and used the day as a dress-rehearsal. It was fantastic with home-made presents and cards and a fab lunch with a huge chocolate cake. I felt like a real diva for the day and loved every minute of it and because everything went so brilliantly, it made us all feel a lot more confident about offering our services to the public. By the end of August, Mum was booked up until Valentine's Day the following year.

We all pitched in at the weekends.

Mum is managing director and chief cake maker.

I am creative director (or as my brothers call me, Miss Bossy Boots.) I do all the table designs, menus and invites.

Will and his mates do the entertainment (or as I say, dress up in mad clothes and act stupid.)

Uncle Kev is in charge of transport.

Auntie Pat and Phoebe help Mum with the catering.

Andrea researches themes and keeps the bookings and accounts.

Dan is prime cake taster and tea maker.

I never did get to go to Italy with the other Crazy Maisies but in the end, I didn't mind. While they were there, they texted me every day and took so many pics on their digital cameras that I felt that I had been there with them.

Best of all though, I finally understood what Dr Cronus and Nessa had been on about. I learnt about acceptance by seeing and appreciating what I had. Not what I hadn't.

And that has made all the difference.

I'm honest about everything now both with my family and my friends. I even told Mum about how I felt that Dad leaving was my fault. She was so shocked and reassured me that no way was it because of me. She said that they hadn't been getting on for a long *long* time and that part of the reason that he didn't leave earlier was because of Andrea, Will, Dan and I. She said he never was much good at communicating his feelings and that was part of their problem. When she said that, it made me think how important it is to tell the people that you love that you care about them and let them in on what's going on in your head, both good and bad.

It's funny because at the beginning of the month, when my time as a Zodiac Girl started happening, I thought that something cosmic or way-out was going to happen that would change my life forever. But it's been quieter than that. Nothing extraterrestrial or weird, just a shift in my attitude. Like I'm myself with my mates now. My real self.

And that has made all the difference.

I often see the planet guys in Osbury and we always stop for a chat and a catch up. Nessa and Uri are my favourites and they have been really helpful in helping me with a personal project – and that's making a business out of my greeting cards. Nessa gave me all her top tips on how to make them look original and pretty (the way she did the messages she sent me). Uri showed me how I can use all the latest technology to incorporate Nessa's ideas and get images from the web. I make all sorts of special occasion cards and last week, I had a stall at a craft market. Georgie, Hannah and Megan helped me man the stall and we sold every single card. Uri loves them too and ordered a whole pile to sell in the cyber café!

Next year when there's a school trip, one thing's for sure and that is that I will be going along with the rest of the Crazy Maisies. And I'll have earned my place on the trip with my own money!

My month as Zodiac Girl is long over but I'll never forget it. Or them. Meeting them made me realize that life can be extraordinary and not because someone is born wealthy or has more than someone else. What makes a life extraordinary is the people in it. Family and friends.

And I've got the best of both.

The Taurus Files
Characteristics, Facts and Fun.

Apr 21 - May 21

Calm and considerate, Taureans make good and loyal friends. But there's another side to this sign – Taureans like material possessions and beautiful things. They've often got their eye on some new designer clothes, expensive food or five-star treatment of one type or another.

Taureans are very practical, but can also be stubborn and lazy. Normally chilled out, they don't like arguing, but if they are really pushed they can explode. So, if you see a storm brewing over a Taurean head you should run for cover!

Element:	Earth
Colour:	Green, pale blue, purple
Birthstone:	Emerald
Animal:	Bull
Lucky day:	Friday
Planet:	ruled by Venus

Taurus best friends are likely to be:
Virgo
Capricorn

Taurus enemies are likely to be:
Aries
Gemini
Leo

A Taurean's idea of heaven would be:
A glamorous lunch followed by a super shopping spree – all paid for by someone else.

A Taurus would go mad if:
They had a job where they had to hurry and rush the whole time.

Famous Taureans:
Cher
Andre Agassi
Fred Astaire
Jack Nicholson
Florence Nightingale
Uma Thurman

Here's the first chapter of another brilliant
Zodiac Girls story, **Brat Princess**.

Chapter One
Welcome to my world

"No. I am not ready. Do I look like I'm ready?"

I was lying on a sun lounger by the pool at our villa in St Kitts in the Caribbean, my mobile in one hand, a chocolate milkshake in the other. Coco was lying on the sunbed next to mine, also wearing shades. She's my dog – a pink Bisson-Frisse. (Everyone at my last school had a dinky dog but no-one had had theirs dyed the way I had. I had to do something – all the pooches looked the same, white and cute but now Coco stands out in a crowd and matches my new nail colour *perfectly*.)

I'd just been thinking how utterly cool life was here on this paradise island when I was interrupted by a demand as to whether I was ready to leave. Anyone with half a brain should have been able to see that I was no way prepared to board a flight to Europe. Like what kind of idiot would travel to Paris in a turquoise bikini? Even if it is from Prada's new collection and on everyone's must have list for the season? We used to live in England when I was younger so I know how cold it can get over in that part of the world. Like, Brrrfreezingville.

"Sorry Miss Hedley-Dent but…" whinged Henry. (He's my dad's chauffeur, PA and handyman though you'd hardly know it. In his usual garb of Bermuda shorts and Hawaiian shirt and with his shoulder length blond hair, he looks more like a professional surfer than a servant.)

"What now Henry?" I was beginning to feel cross and would have been more snappy if it wasn't for the fact that my friend Tigsy was on hold, waiting for me, on the other end of the phone.

"Just er… the plane has been ready for some time and the pilot has been waiting for you for over an hour."

"So? Tell him that he may have to wait *another* hour because I am not ready and I want to catch some more rays before I leave."

"May I at least give him some idea of when you may be ready for take off?"

I gave Henry my best withering look. Tigs and I'd practised it for ages in the mirror at school last year before I got expelled. One eyebrow up, nostrils breathed in and lips tight. Tigsy said that I appeared more constipated than cross when I did the 'look' but, whatever, Henry got the message, backed out of the room and closed the door. He's so pathetic when he does that droning on thing. Like timetables… airports… Like it's my problem. Not.

At last I could resume my call. I lay back on the lounger, took a sip of my milkshake and *erg*hhh… I spat out the shake. It was *LUKE*WARM!

"Shirla. SHIRLA," I called.

A few minutes later, Shirla, our Caribbean housekeeper came out from the house. She always does everything sooo slowly. Like it's all one mighty effort. Probably due to the fact that she is about five million stone heavy. She's like a house on legs. Legs that are made of jelly - she doesn't so much walk as wobble her way along. I pointed at the glass. "More ice. And a dab more of that yummy chocolate."

"Oo you likes the chocolate. If you not careful girl, you going to become one big melted chocolate in that sun," she said as she swayed over, took the glass then waddled off towards the kitchen.

"Oh and can you get Mason to do me some chips before the flight takes off. Those big square ones he does. And bring a little pot of that scrummy sour cream and chives to dunk in. And something for Coco." (Mason's our cook and Shirla's husband. They're an odd couple, he's as skinny as she is large.)

Shirla stopped for a moment. "Uhuh, I guess I could," she said, "but you ought to eat some greens one of these days or else them spots on your chin there are going to be breaking out all over your pretty little face. And don't you go giving that dog no chocolate neither. It ain't right." She tutted to herself then disappeared inside before I could say anything.

I picked up the phone again.

"Yum. Chips," said Tigsy at the other end. "Think I'll get our maid to do me some. I lurve chips."

"Sorry Tigs, guess you heard all that? Like, welcome to my world. Can you believe it? Henry trying to tell *me* when we have to leave, like, who pays who round here?"

"Exactement," said Tigsy. "You have to let them know who's boss yeah?"

"Yeah. It's Mummy's fault. She's way too nice with them all. Like a little mouse. She's like, er, pardon me for squeaking. And Dad's never here so what can one expect? It's left to me to let them know who's in charge like I haven't got enough to do as it is."

"Totally."

I stared out over the infinity pool and the sea beyond. It was glistening with a thousand tiny stars in the afternoon sun. "Yeah. Like sometimes I think that just because I'm only fourteen, they, like, think they can tell me what to do. But I say, no way. No way."

"Yeah. No way. Er but Leonora, I'm not being difficult or anything but one thing I do know and that is that sometimes when travelling, like, doing a strop can work against you. Like, it's the beginning of December, coming up to Christmas yeah?"

"Yeah. Like, deck the halls with Christmas holly, blah de blah de blah, de blah de yawn."

"So everyone's on the move, yeah? Not just us?"

"I guess."

"Well I know from when Daddy does his own bookings for coming into land in our ickle jet, if you miss your slot, particularly at busy times, you don't get another."

"Oh. Un problemo you think? So you're saying what exactly?"

Tigsy laughed at the other end of the phone. "That you'd better get your stonkingly rich butt off that island in the Caribbean, Leonora Hedley-Dent, and onto the jet or else we're not going to be able to do our shopping trip in Paris and get back in time for Christmas."

"Like I care about Christmas. Hah bumhug to all that, I say, it's just *another* excuse for the staff to skive off for the day," I said but I did get up, slip my feet into my Gucci mules with the kitten heels and make my way through the open French doors to my bedroom. Coco got up and followed me. She's sooooo cute. She walks like she's wearing heels too.

"I know," said Tigsy. "Three weeks to go and it will all be one big bore as usual. The fun part will be you being here and the shopping beforehand although there will be presents on the day. Daddy said he might get me a new diamond Cartier watch this year. I've put it on the list as I am getting tired of my Rolex. It's so last season. But really Lee Lee, I mean, I'm going to be okay for getting to Paris. I'm in Geneva and only have to hop on a train to get there.'

"It's cool. I get you. I'll get a move on," I said as I took a couple of chocolate bars out of a drawer and flung them into the suitcase on the bed. "I'm packing as we speak but I'm not going to let Henry think that I'm doing it for him."

'No. Course not. But do hurry. I've got no-one to plaaaay with over here."

"I'll see you soon."

"Excellent. Kissy kissy. Daddy's booked us the whole of the top floor at the George the Fifth hotel. I've been there before when Imelda Parker Knowles had her sixteenth birthday bash there in the summer. It's utterly dinky. I think you'll like it."

"Sorreee. Packing. Be there. Bysie bye."

"Bysie bye."

I put my phone down by the bed and went to the mirror, spritzed on some of my Goddess perfume, picked up my brush and brushed my hair through. I was pleased with the way it was looking. The sun had made my new blonde highlights even lighter. One day, Shirla caught me before I'd used my hair straighteners. She said that I had fabulous hair. Hah! She has no idea of the work it takes to keep it looking good. Like, I would be mortified if anyone saw me with my hair in its natural state (curly wurly) but she said that it suited my birth sign, which is Leo. My hair, which is half way down my back, is like a tawny lion's mane. *Huh. Like why exactly would I want to look like a lion for heaven's sake?* I thought as I applied a slick of mascara. *Most of them have manky manes, hardly the honey and fudge organic highlights that Daniel Blake, stylist to the stars, runs through mine!*

I put in my blue eye contacts to cover my boring brown, applied some concealer over my spots and glanced round to see what else needed to be done. Coco was watching my every move.

"Oh don't look at me like that boo boo," I said. "I'll only be gone a few days."

Coco rolled over on her back and wriggled on the bed. She's sooo sweet even if her tummy is a different colour to the rest of her. (I ran out of dye.)

Mummy and Shirla had done most of my packing but I threw a few more things in, just in case. All essentials that they'd missed. Lip gloss. Latest chill out CD. More choccie bars for emergencies. I glanced over at the photo in a silver frame by my bed. *Mustn't forget to pack that*, I thought. I never went anywhere without it. It was of me and Poppy, my sister. It was taken when I was twelve and she was ten. Oh. Hair straighteners. I threw them in on top. I couldn't believe they'd forgotten them, although actually yeah – I could, another example of how nobody around here has a clue about what matters to me. To travel without them would be like being without an arm or a leg, they're that important. It was hard to know what else I'd need though. Tigsy said it was unseasonably warm in Europe but it wouldn't be as hot as it was here on St Kitts. The only clothes that I'd worn for the last week were bikinis and sarongs. Still. If it got too cold, I could buy a new set of cashmere. I'd worn the ones I got last December at least three times in the winter season so I was well due for new ones.

I pulled my fave pair of skinny jeans out of the cupboard and began to put them on. Erg. Arff. They were meant to be tight but not that tight!

"MUMMY!!!!"

Mummy appeared at the door a few seconds later. "Yes darling?"

"My jeans! They've shrunk."

Mummy came in and watched me struggling to get the jeans done up.

"Er… you don't think darling, that you could have maybe put on a teensy weensy bit of weight do you?"

I could feel a tantrum coming on. I could feel it in the pit of my stomach bubbling and boiling like a volcano about to erupt, like, it was all right for her, she never put on an ounce of fat no matter what she ate.

She was so lucky with her straight blonde hair and her perfect figure. She didn't look her age either and people always thought we were sisters. As if. It soooo wasn't fair that I'd inherited Dad's frump genes and his stupid curly hair rather than hers. "Me? Put on weight! These are MY BEST JEANS. I HAD TO WAIT THREE MONTHS ON A LIST FOR THEM TO COME IN TO THE SHOP AND THAT DOPEY DORA OF A HOUSEKEEPER HAS GONE AND SHRUNK THEM IN THE WASH!"

For a split second, I swear I saw a hint of a smile cross Mummy's face which made me madder. She put her hand on my arm. "Now calm down," she said in a soft voice that made me want to hit something. "You're a growing girl…"

I brushed her hand away. "Calm DOWN? Growing GIRL? I CAN'T GROW ANY MORE. I'M *ENORMOUS AS IT IS*."

Mummy sighed. "You've got a lovely figure Leonora and fabulous long legs, you're…"

"WHAT DO YOU KNOW? I'M ALREADY A SIZE TEN AND EVERYONE IN MY CLASS IS A SIX OR A FOUR! And Lottie James is even a size ZERO! I'M AN ELEPHANT! MY WHOLE DAY HAS BEEN RUINED. I HATE YOU. YOU NEVER UNDERSTAND."

I wriggled out of the jeans. They wouldn't do up no

matter how much I yanked at the zip. I tossed them onto the bed then threw myself, front down, on after them. And then I went for it.

"WaaaaaaARRRRGGHHHHHHHHHHHHHHHH HHHHHHHHHHHH."

I thrashed my arms, pummelled my pillows and threw my legs up and down. And then I felt sick. Yes, I was going to be sick. I could feel it. I sat up. "And now I FEEL SICK."

Mummy looked at me with wide eyes and an expression of terror. *Why oh why couldn't she ever say or do the right thing when I feel like this?* I wondered. *I'm sure I'm adopted. I can't be her daughter. We're nothing like each other and she hasn't got a clue what to do with me.* My head started to throb. "And now I've got a headache coming," I wailed. "And I'm fat. And spotty. And it's all your FAULT!"

At that moment, there was a gentle knock at the door and Henry put his head round. I picked up a pillow and threw it at him.

"GET OUT! GET OUT. ALL OF YOU. OUT. *OUT.* I HATE YOU ALL."

Henry disappeared mega fast and Mummy scurried out like a frightened rabbit.

"WahurggghhhhhhhhhHHHH," I yelled at the ceiling. "*No-one* understands me. Not *anyone*. I *hate* everyone. I hate them all. I hate my life. I'm so ugly. And *fat*. I am soooooooooooo unhappy."